Davi

Try and Try Again

SALZWASSER
VERLAG

David Alfred Doudney

Try and Try Again

Reprint of the original, first published in 1864.

1st Edition 2022 | ISBN: 978-3-75259-546-8

Verlag (Publisher): Salzwasser Verlag GmbH, Zeilweg 44, 60439 Frankfurt, Deutschland
Vertretungsberechtigt (Authorized to represent): E. Roepke, Zeilweg 44, 60439 Frankfurt, Deutschland
Druck (Print): Books on Demand GmbH, In de Tarpen 42, 22848 Norderstedt, Deutschland

TRY

AND

TRY AGAIN

BEING

AN OUTLINE OF THE LIVES OF TWO YOUTHS WHO BECAME CLERGYMEN OF THE CHURCH OF ENGLAND.

BY "OLD JONATHAN."

"ONCE OR TWICE THOUGH YOU SHOULD FAIL,
TRY, TRY, TRY AGAIN.
IF YOU WOULD AT LAST PREVAIL,
TRY, TRY, TRY AGAIN.
IF WE STRIVE, 'TIS NO DISGRACE,
THOUGH WE MAY NOT WIN THE RACE;
WHAT SHOULD YOU DO IN THAT CASE?
TRY, TRY, TRY AGAIN."

Eighth Thousand.

LONDON

1864.

PREFACE.

A PORTION of this work has already been presented to the public, and met with a large and most encouraging demand. The call for another edition has induced the author materially to add to its contents. The totally-changed position of one closely identified with the facts detailed in the following pages, as contrasted with that he occupied when the former editions of this work were issued, open up a course of events calculated in the highest degree, under God, to stimulate and encourage the efforts of those on whose behalf the work was specially written.

The narrative, as repeatedly intimated, is strictly matter of fact. It is simple and straightforward. It has neither colour nor flourish.

As the reader advances in the perusal of this volume, and especially as he draws near to its close, he will find ample means of confirmation. He will know to what quarter to look for another, among the ten thousand examples which present themselves upon the page of real life, for evidence and illustration of the fact, that Jehovah ratifies His word, "I love them that love me; and those that seek me early, shall find me;" that Wisdom's "ways are ways of pleasantness, and all her paths are peace;" that "Godliness is profitable unto all things, having promise of the life that now is, and of that which is to come."

That this humble production may be a means, in the hands of God the Holy Ghost, of leading some dear young readers to cast in their lot among the people of God, is indeed the author's heartfelt desire. The Lord, in mercy, grant that they, with Mary, may "choose that good part which shall not be taken away" from them; with Moses, choose "rather to suffer affliction with the people of God, than to enjoy the pleasures of sin for a season, esteeming the reproach (for) Christ greater riches than the treasures in Egypt; for he had respect unto the recompence of the reward." Then, not only will their course be satisfactory on earth, but

> "After death their joys shall be
> Lasting as eternity."

November, 1863.

CHILDREN'S TEA MEETING
ST. LUKE'S CHURCH
INDUSTRIAL PRESS
ST. LUKE'S SCHOOLS
ST. LUKE'S CHURCH

CONTENTS.

INTRODUCTION.

JONATHAN—HIS BOYHOOD—HIS MOTTO—THOUGHTS, GOOD AND BAD—ABOUT TO TRY—IS IT RIGHT?—THE BROKEN WINDOW—CONFESSION—THE PROUD BOY AND THE HALFPENNY ERRAND—THE SHORTNESS OF TIME—PATIENCE AND PERSEVERANCE.

AS I was once young myself, I am about to try and write something for those who are young now. Though getting old, I can remember a good deal of what I used to think and feel when I was young. And I dare say, as hearts are so much alike, you, my young reader, think and feel just as I used to do.

Hence I will write what I hope, under God, may be of use to you. But at the outset I would have you know that what I am going to tell you is all strictly *true*.

Well now, as it is usual with ministers to take a text as a sort of starting-post, I think I cannot do better than take one. But my text is to be very short. Young people, you know, are not fond of long texts, as they have often to repeat them when they get home, or at school next day. T—R—Y! That's my text.

I.—T. *T* stands for *Thought.* I need not tell you, for I am sure you know it, that there are many kinds of thought. There are good thoughts and bad thoughts. Thoughts that come from God, and thoughts that come from Satan, and our own wicked hearts. There are thoughts about time, and thoughts about eternity. Thoughts for the body, and thoughts for the soul. Angry thoughts and peaceful thoughts. Selfish thoughts, or thoughts about what we shall get and have; generous thoughts, or how we can help others. But out of the many thoughts which pass and repass the mind, it is one kind of thought of which I want now to speak. It is that sort of thought which boys have when they hear or read of others. They hear or they read of men who have been useful and happy, and, what some people call, great men; and they think, "Ah, but they never were as I am. They must have had what I have not. They had good homes, or great friends, or plenty of money, or what not; and all this was the secret of their success. This was why they became such useful and happy men." Now, dear boys, these are very wrong thoughts; for, in most cases, those who have become great and good men, had not, as boys, what you speak of. For too often when boys have good homes (as they are called), or great friends, or plenty of money, they think they need not give heed to our text—TRY.

II. R. *R* stands for *Right*. When we are about to try to do this or to do that, it is well to *think*. "Is it right?" And, as it is hard to know now and then whether to go here or there, to do this or that, is *right*, think of and repeat over these four short words, "THOU, GOD, SEEST ME." This will be almost sure to decide the matter. And, if helped to do what is *right*, take my word for it you will be a ten times happier boy than if you take your own way, and do what is *wrong*. I will tell you why. I knew a boy once to throw a stone—a very bad practice, mark—and with that stone he broke a window. It was dark, and he ran away. But he thought, "Is this *right?* Should I like any one to serve me the same?" So he went to the shop, and told the person who kept it that it was *he* who had broken the window. Now it was at first quite a task—really an effort—to do this; but he was all the happier afterwards. He could not have passed that shop without thinking of the broken pane, if he had not gone and done what was *right*. It is much the easiest and much the best way. Again, I knew a boy once who had a very proud heart; he thought a great deal too much of what others thought of him. But one day he was put to a very severe test. His master sent him upon an errand. It was to go to a shop in a very fine street, where a great many ladies and gentlemen used to deal, and to ask the shopkeeper for a *halfpenny* which his master said he owed him. The boy walked up that fine street, and, thinking what he had to do, said to himself, "I'd sooner pay the *halfpenny* myself a dozen times over; but would it be *right?* Did not my master send me? Are not his commands all the same, whether it is for a penny or a pound?" So, feeling it was *right,* into the shop he went; and, when asked what was wanted, said, his master had sent him for a *halfpenny*. It was a *trial,* but it was a *triumph,* too. Why?—It was *right.*

III. Y.. *Y* stands for *Years*. A *year* seems a long time when 365 days have to come and go before it ends; and when five, or ten, or fifteen years have to pass away ere such things as boys set their minds upon can be had, they are apt to want patience, and to say, "Oh, it's no good to think of it. Why should I *try?* What's the use?" This is anything but *right,* and too often leads to what is *wrong*. If, on the other hand, the mind was set, first, to *think,* and, secondly, to *do* what was *right,* it is strange how quickly months and years seem to glide away.

Well now, having given a few thoughts upon my

text I shall proceed to *proof*. I shall show, from plain matter of fact, that it *is* of use to TRY; and this will bring us to our first chapter.

CHAPTER I.

ALFRED AND JOHN—UNCLE AND NEPHEW—THEIR EARLY DAYS, AND HOW THEY CAME TO LIVE TOGETHER—THE SICK-BED—THE DYING MOTHER SO HAPPY—THE HYMN—THE BEREAVED HUSBAND—GOES TO SEA—JOHN'S SORROW—ALFRED'S SYMPATHY—THEIR FRIENDSHIP—DEATH OF RICHARD AND LOUISA—THEIR FUNERAL—THE LITTLE MOURNERS.

THERE lived some years ago two little boys—not brothers—but though there was only a year and a half between them in age they stood related to each other as uncle and nephew. It seemed very strange at first to hear the younger salute his companion with "Uncle this," and "Uncle that," but this, after a time, he discontinued; and each called the other by his Christian name. Well, though they were not brothers, still they lived in the same family, and were born under the same roof; and I will tell you how this happened. When John (that is, the younger) was about four years old, his mamma was taken very ill. He had then a younger brother, named

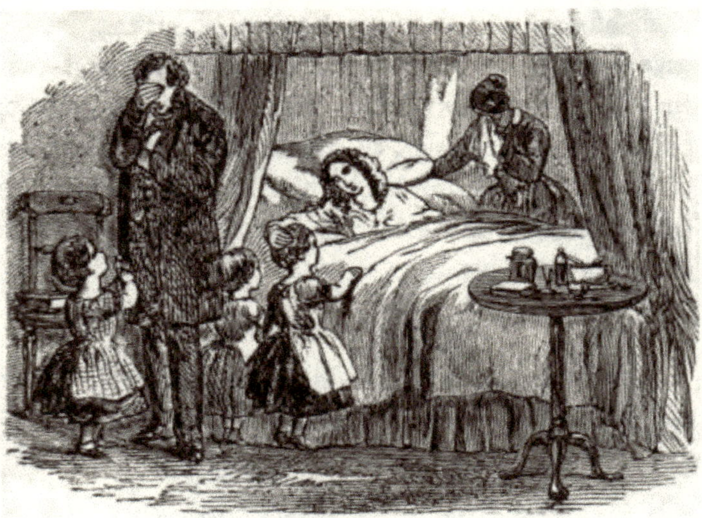

Richard, and a little sister—quite a babe—named Louisa. Soon after this babe was born, his mamma became so weak and delicate, that fears were entertained about her recovery; and, alas! these fears proved to be correct. She grew worse and worse—weaker and weaker—until at length she died. But hers, as far as she was concerned, was a happy sick-bed, and a joyful death; for, with the great Apostle Paul, she could say,

"I know whom I have believed, and am persuaded that He is able to keep that which I have committed to Him against that day." Look at the engraving.

There is John's dear mamma upon her sick-bed; his papa weeping; John looking up with an expression of "Don't cry, papa!" Alfred and little Richard on one side of the bed; and Jane—a faithful nurse, of whom I shall afterwards have to speak—on the other. I will give you a proof that she was happy, though she knew that her end was very near. Her husband was standing by her bedside one day, as well as some other members of her family. Addresssing him in her usually affectionate manner, she said, "My dear, I wish you would sing that sweet hymn,

"'On Jordan's stormy banks I stand.'"

"I will *read* it to you, my dear," was his reply; "but our hearts are too *sad* to *sing* it:" and then he read those touching lines:—

"On Jordan's stormy banks I stand,
And cast a wishful eye
To Canaan's fair and happy land,
Where my possessions lie.

"Oh the transporting, rapturous scene
That rises to my sight!
Sweet fields arrayed in living green,
And rivers of delight.

"O'er all those wide-extended plains
Shines one eternal day;
There God the Sun for ever reigns,
And scatters night away.

"No chilling winds or poisonous breath
Can reach that healthful shore,—
Sickness and sorrow, pain and death,
Are felt and feared no more.

"When shall I reach that happy place,
And be for ever blest?
When shall I see my Father's face,
And in His bosom rest?

"Filled with delight, my raptured soul
Could here no longer stay;
Though Jordan's waves around me roll
Fearless I'd launch away."

I cannot but add, may you, my dear boys, and I, have the same heart-cheering prospect when brought into the same circumstances.

Well, as I said, John's mamma died; and, after she was gone, the house was so gloomy, and everything so bespoke his sad, sad loss, that John's papa resolved to give up house-keeping, and once more go to sea. His furniture was, therefore, sold off; the house closed; and John and his little brother and sister went to reside with their grandparents. It was here that John and Alfred became so closely united. No two youths could be dearer to each other than were these. Morning, noon, and night, found them side by side—heart was entwined about heart; they were *as one;* most near and dear. John's papa going to sea again was deeply trying, not only to himself, but to his whole circle of kindred and acquaintance. Scarcely had he time to recover from the shock of that sad separation from one so tenderly and deservedly loved, ere he felt it his duty to separate also from those who had hitherto so cheered his little circle. It was a mournful day when John's papa bade him a long farewell, and, embarking at Portsmouth, sailed for Jamaica. He knew the uncertainty of life, and felt that he might soon be called to bear further painful losses.

Here is John's papa shaking hands with his father-in-law (Alfred's father); and John and Alfred at their feet; whilst an uncle takes Richard upon his knee.

Alfred saw the sorrow of John on account of his papa's departure, and he resolved, as far as in him lay, to make up the loss. Whatever they had been before, they were to be still more devoted now. They were to be bosom-friends indeed. They walked and talked by day, and by night were deep in conversation long after they had retired to rest. They had a tolerable share of toys; but their delight, for most part, was in books. The Book of books was ever near them, and in their bedroom were three long shelves, well filled with volumes of history and narrarive.

But, as though their attachment was as yet incomplete, another circumstance arose to cement the bond of union, and to bind them (if possible) yet closer to each other. Richard (John's brother) one day was taken very ill, and died. Here was another void, which made John turn to Alfred, as if to say, "Make up this further loss." Three days had scarcely elapsed, ere Louisa (the babe) was seized, and she died too. There, at either end of the sofa, lay these precious ones, lovely in the sleep of death. Many went to the house of mourning, to gaze upon a scene so touching. But one now remained of that interesting trio—but one of a group about which a father's love and a mother's tender devotion had so entwined.

Once again the mourners meet—and the coaches come to carry to a mother's grave the sacred relics of her offspring. One they were in life, and scarcely in death divided. See those two devoted youths, as they sit side by side, upon their mournful mission. What are their words—what their reflections—as they gaze upon those tiny coffins, and listen to the measured tread of horses? What means that deep-toned bell? What this halt? What this procession? What those solemn words, as they echo o'er these tombs, "I am the resurrection and the life?" What this open grave? What that hollow sound, as "earth to earth, ashes to ashes, dust to dust," drop upon the ear?

CHAPTER II.

YOUTH THE BEST TIME TO SUFFER—DISCIPLINE A GOOD BEGINNING OF LIFE—PRODUCES THOUGHT AND CAREFULNESS—THE SPOILED SON—HIS EXTRAVAGANCE AND AFTER-FALL—HIS FATHER DIES—THE RICH MERCHANT—INDULGED CHILDREN—HIS DEATH—THEIR FORTUNES—THEIR FAILURE—THE FOLLY OF LOOKING TO FRIENDS—THE ADVANTAGE OF SELF-RELIANCE—THE BOOK OF PROVERBS AND ITS CLAIMS—THE SWEETS OF WISDOM.

MY last chapter was sad. It could not be otherwise. Had I drawn a veil over the facts there mentioned, I should have failed to show the nature and groundwork of the union that existed between John and Alfred. I hope in my present, but especially in my future chapters, to take a more cheering view of the course these two youths were to pursue. It is said in the Scriptures that "it is good that a man bear the yoke in his youth." By which I understand it is well that in his early days he should have such tests and such trials as should lead him to form a just view of life, and that he might then know for himself what the world is, and what he might expect in passing through it. If the days of youth were all sunshine, and clouds never obscured his fair heavens, he would form opinions of life so bright and so promising, that disappointment must follow. Thousands are thus deceived, and hence lay the foundation of future restlessness and discontent. Whereas, if in their early days they have been sobered by *care*, thoughtfulness and caution may be looked for as a good result.

Perhaps a simple example will best explain this.

JONATHAN knew a youth—an only son—whose father being in what is termed easy circumstances, and very indulgent, he was in the habit of receiving all he wanted. His every wish was granted. However large or extravagant his desires, they were always complied with. With either himself or his sister, it was only to ask and have. Nought was denied them. Their youthful life was one continuous scene of *indulgence*. The youth especially knew nothing of denial or restraint. At last he was sent out into the world. He was placed to a profession. As he advanced in years, his claims were larger and more frequent. His father was at length no longer able to supply his wants. The young man thus, for the first time, disappointed, rebelled. His father soon after died; and he whom (under God) prudence and care might have directed into a thoughtful course, speedily

became a wanderer and a vagabond. Had he "borne the yoke is his youth," very different might have been the issue!

JONATHAN was also acquainted with a large and at one time respectable family. The head of it had been very successful as a merchant. His children were much indulged. Self-denial was little, if at all, known in that family circle. At length the parent died; and, when his property—large as it was in itself—came to be divided among some twelve or thirteen children, £2,200 or £1,500 each was but a small sum to sport with. The same expensive habits were indulged, until each and every one was reduced to within a state of pauperism. Had the several members of this large household "borne the yoke in their youth," they had known better how to have taken care of the little wealth which, well applied, might have made them comfortable for the residue of their days.

The looking too much to parents, rich uncles and aunts, or kind relatives and friends, is most injurious. JONATHAN would affectionately caution his young friends against this. It crushes that *self-reliance* which, as a human means, is so necessary to cherish. It is an old saying, and contains a great deal of truth, "God helps the man who helps himself." It is "the diligent soul is made fat;" and this is applicable to things of time as well as to those of eternity.

In keeping with these remarks, JONATHAN would urge upon his dear young readers the careful perusal of the Book of Proverbs. The sayings of the wise Man (if stored up in the heart) may be a great help as well as a timely preservative. "My son," says Solomon, "despise not the chastening of the Lord, neither be weary of His correction (this is, to bear the yoke in his youth); for whom the Lord loveth He correcteth, even as a father the son in whom he delighteth. Happy is the man that findeth wisdom, and the man that getteth understanding. for the merchandize of it is better than the merchandize of silver, and the gain thereof than fine gold. She is more precious than rubies: and all the things thou canst desire are not to be compared unto her. Length of days is in her right hand; and in her left hand riches and honour. Her ways are ways of pleasantness, and all her paths are peace. She is a tree of life to them that lay hold upon her; and happy is every one that retaineth her. The Lord by wisdom hath founded the earth: by understanding hath He established the heavens. By His knowledge the depths are broken up, and the clouds drop down the dew. My son, let not them depart from thine eyes: keep sound wisdom and discretion; so shall they be life unto thy soul, and grace to thy neck. Then shalt thou walk in thy way safely, and thy foot shall not stumble. When thou liest down, thou shalt not be afraid; vea, thou shalt lie down, and thy sleep shall be sweet."

CHAPTER III.

THE STUDY OF THE SCRIPTURES—THE NURSE—HER MISTRESS'S DYING WORD—JANE LOVES HER MEMORY—SHE READS—IS BLESSED—PRAYS WITH AND FOR HER YOUTHFUL CHARGE—THE BLESSING OF A PRAYING SERVANT—THE GODLY STEP-SISTER AND AUNT—HER INFLUENCE UPON THE YOUTHFUL MIND—THE AFFLICTION, ITS INFLUENCE—THE VOICE OF FACT—MARTIAL MUSIC—THE SOLDIER'S FUNERAL—THOUGHTS OF HEAVEN—ALFRED AND JOHN—THEIR CHEERFULNESS—HOME COMFORTS AND HOME PLEASURES GOOD AS A PRESERVATIVE.

IN his last chapter Jonathan recommended to his youthful reader the reading of the Scriptures. It has reminded him of a touching scene at the death of John's beloved mamma. Her last request to the nurse was expressed in these words, *"Jane, read your Bible."* Jane loved her mistress; and, when she was no more, often thought of her dying wish. She gave heed to it. She did read her Bible day by day; and from that time forward, the fruits of that reading were to be seen. As she followed the motherless children to their new home, often would Jane take Alfred and John to her own room, and, bending the knee in prayer, would entreat the Lord to bless them. She was earnest and fervent. Prayer with her was no mere duty, but a privilege. She felt it good to be able to go and pour out her sorrows and her wants into the ears of Him who hath said, "Call upon me in the day of trouble, I will deliver thee, and thou shalt glorify me;" "Acknowledge Him in all thy ways, and He shall direct thy paths." There is not a doubt that Jane's prayers were heard on behalf of herself and the youths of whom she had the charge.

Oh, what a blessing is a praying servant! How many a dear youth has had to date his first serious impressions to the counsel and the care of a prayerful domestic!

But Alfred and John were favoured also in another respect. Not only had they godly parents and grandparents, but the step-sister of Alfred and aunt of John was a godly person too, and she, for a time, undertook the education of these youths. Doubtless to her kind solicitude was to be traced, in a measure, their early formation of character. Her devotion to their interests was extreme. The repeated afflictions and bereavements with which the family had been so painfully familiar, gave tone to her counsel, and tended in no small degree to confirm her statements. It was no mere matter of hearsay.

It was not that such and such things had occurred, or perchance might occur, but there was the presence of the fact. And, as they lived in the outskirts of a large naval and military town, and just at the close of a long and eventful war, how would the frequent sound of martial music, or the witnessing of a soldier's funeral, arouse reflection, and carry the mind even of those youths into the world where many near and dear to them had entered. These various circumstances combined, tended much to check and control that over-elatedness of spirit which is so common in youth.

The reader must not, however, imagine that Alfred and John were dull, and lacking cheerfulness. Such was far from being the case. They had their set hours for study, and between those hours abundant recreation. Being so nearly of an age—related to each other—and brought together under such peculiar circumstances, there was a oneness of taste and feeling, which was a source of ever-new delight. Home was their citadel; they cared not for out-door companions; hence bad associations were avoided, and an immensity of evil saved.

Alfred and John had cause for thankfulness in that all reasonable sources of home-pleasure were afforded them. Parents and guardians might save themselves much after-sorrow, and the objects of their care many a snare, by making home as attractive as possible. Alfred and John had their play-ground as well as their play-room; they had also their little poultry-yard, and niche in the flower-garden, as well as a bed for mustard-and-cress, or early radishes. In their little garden, on one occasion, they planted some laburnum seeds; from these sprang two lovely trees, one of which still flourishes as a memento of those early days.

CHAPTER IV.

DIFFERENCE OF DISPOSITION—JOHN HASTY, BUT MORE PRUDENT—HIS SELF-GOVERNMENT—ALFRED TIMID, BUT THOUGHTLESS—CURIOSITY DANGEROUS—NEED OF SHUNNING THE VERY APPEARANCE OF EVIL—THEIR VISIT TO DEVONSHIRE—THE RAMBLE—SOLDIERS AND THEIR COMPANIONS—THE TEMPTATION—ALFRED'S INDISCRETION—JOHN'S FIRMNESS AND AFFECTIONATE REPROOF—THE DANGER OF GOING IN THE WAY OF EVIL—BOTH PRESERVATION FROM SIN, AND PARDON FOR SIN, ASCRIBED TO GOD.

YOUNG and closely united as these two devoted youths were, a difference of temperament was soon perceptible. John was far before Alfred in strength of mind and fixedness of purpose. It is true that he had a hasty temper, and an occasional outbreak of that temper involved him in many after-regrets. He saw and felt how wrong was the indulgence of passion, and never did a youth more earnestly struggle with himself. He was ever on the watch; and there cannot be a doubt that his keen sense of right and wrong, and the early discovery of his own personal weakness and infirmity, led to that caution and prompt avoidance of evil which so strikingly marked his riper years. On the other hand, Alfred, though deeply sensitive, and the subject of timidity and fear to an unusual degree, was less watchful, and much more easily led astray. There was a curiosity and inquisitiveness about him which led him to hover about and parley with temptation, where John, with the utmost promptitnde, would have exclaimed, "How can I do this great wickedness, and sin against God?"

The after-career of these youths was widely different. Alfred encountered tenfold more suffering than John: and to the fact just mentioned may be ascribed the distinction. Hence JONATHAN would urge upon his dear young friends the "abstaining from all appearance of evil." True it is, that Alfred, in common with John, was singularly preserved, and in both was verified the gracious assurance,—"Train up a child in the way he should go, and when he is old he will not depart from it;" but of Alfred, it may be said, notwithstanding, he was "saved by the skin of his teeth." Into many and many a snare did his own incaution, want of firmness, and idle curiosity lead him, where John would have rushed from the very first approach of the tempter. One simple fact will prove this. Alfred and John were one Midsummer upon a visit in Devonshire. They were now youths of 15 to 17, or thereabouts. One day they were walking round the sea-coast, very near some large barracks, when, upon a turn of the road, they suddenly fell in with a number of soldiers and their abandoned companions. Instantly these shouted, and charged the youths with cowardice. Alfred halted, but John walked on; and presently, when Alfred came up with him, "Alfred," said John, "it was wrong to have stopped;" and so it was. Much evil might have been the consequence. It was, to say the least, a partial yielding to temptation. Alfred, in too great a measure, forgot the injunction, "My son, if sinners entice thee, consent thou not;" "My son, walk thou not in the way with them; refrain thy foot from their path" (Prov. i. 10, 15). "Enter not into the path of the wicked, and go not in the way of evil. Avoid it, pass not by it, turn from it, and pass away." "Let thine eyes look right on, and let thine eyelids look straight before thee. Ponder the path of thy feet, and let all thy ways be established. Turn not to the right hand, nor to the left: remove thy foot from evil" (Prov. iv. 14, 15). Much, as has been intimated, of Alfred's after-anguish—and he had no small portion—may be ascribed to his want of abiding by the golden rule of *shunning the very path of the wicked.* "Can a man take fire in his bosom, and his clothes not be burned? Can one go upon hot coals, and his feet not be burned?" (Prov. vi. 27. 28). Hence both Alfred and John may well argue the point as to which was the greatest debtor to God's free and sovereign grace; John, who had strength to resist the very semblance of sin, or Alfred, who might well again and again say, "My feet were *almost* gone, my steps had *well nigh* slipped?" (Psal. lxxiii. 2). Certain, however, it is, that neither in the one case nor the other was there the slightest cause for boasting; but well might each exclaim, "Not unto us, O Lord, not unto us, but unto Thy name give glory, for Thy mercy, and for Thy truth's sake" (Psal. cxv. 1).

It will, moreover, be found in most cases, that where there is a want of *firmness*, there is a great amount of *fear.* This fear, too, will operate in numberless ways. On two occasions, when very young, this fear showed itself in Alfred: once when attacked by a fowl, and at another time by a dog. John, on the other hand, was far more courageous, because firmer and more decided in his character.

Much allowance must certainly be made for temperament and disposition. One youth is naturally timid, another as naturally fearless; these dispositions, therefore, require different treatment. Where there is an over-amount of courage, bordering upon defiance of danger, *caution* should be the watchword on the part of the teacher; but if, on the other hand, there be a superabundance of fear and timidity, *gentle reasoning* and *remonstrance* are necessary. To a want of discrimination on the part of the instructor, much after-sorrow is to be attributed. Moreover, many a child has been ruined, and fallen a prey to the saddest fears and the most needless apprehensions, through *servants* exciting their imaginations by their ghost-stories and fairy-tales. Nothing can be more reprehensible than conduct of this description, by which many a poor child has been victimized, and rendered little, if anything, better than a wreck during all its after-life. Bad as may be the practice of boy setting upon boy, or endeavouring to excite ill-feeling in the minds of one class of youth against those who may be better circumstanced, or more prudently conducted, such conduct (bad though it be) is not, to JONATHAN's mind at least, nearly so much to be condemned as domestics exercising the most pitiable and contemptible iufluence of exciting fear in the young and tender mind. Alfred was, to a great extent, thus victimized. Natural fear was wrought upon. Hence, where one youth, when necessary, would confront danger, he would at once fall a prey to it. Take, for example, his on one occasion being attacked by a dog. As with horses so with dogs, firmness and determination, coupled with a degree of kindness, will commonly overcome them, when of fear they would take advantage.

CHAPTER V.

THE LOVE OF BOOKS—CHEAP PUBLICATIONS—THEIR INTRODUCTION—MAGAZINE DAY—THE BINDER'S—THE YOUNG BOOKWORMS, AND THE LIBRARY—SUNDAY AFTERNOON READINGS—JUVENILE BIOGRAPHIES AND THEIR SUGGESTIONS—WISH TO BE A MISSIONARY—DESIRES FOR AUTHORSHIP, PRINTING, AND PUBLISHING—THE WELFARE OF OTHERS—SUCH THOUGHTS TO BE CHERISHED—GENERALLY THE FORERUNNER OF GOOD—GOD TO BE ACKNOWLEDGED—THE DISPENSATIONS OF PROVIDENCE—TRY, IN SPITE OF DIFFICULTIES.

I SPOKE in a previous chapter of the love of Alfred and John for books. Above all, however, the Scripture was their choice. At night each placed his Bible under his pillow, that if roused at early morn, they might read. Their books being ranged over the head of their bed, were so much the more accessible. At that time cheap publications were little known. "The Sunday Scholar's Magazine" and "Child's Companion" were among the first cheap issue. These were carefully collected, and in due time bound. The first of the month was looked for with special interest, as that would bring a moderate influx to their library. Their pocket-money was nearly all devoted to the purchase of little books, which being read, and then duly preserved, were, as soon as they could make a good-sized volume, taken off to the nearest binder, to be sewn together and half-bound. And how anxious were Alfred and John for the given time to pass, in order that, upon the promised day, they might call for the newly-bound book. How carefully was it wrapped in paper; how nimble their steps homeward; how general its exhibition through the family circle; how fresh the interest, whilst submitted in the new covering, to another perusal; and, lastly, how attractive in their eyes its appearance, when ranged with red, and brown, and green, upon their book-shelves.

So great was their taste for books, and such was their fondness for reading, that on many a Sunday afternoon, between the hours of service, would Alfred and John be found seated side by side, even in a hay-loft, perusing with deep interest some fresh addition to their library, or volume which had aforetime afforded them instruction and pleasure. Juvenile biographies always gave them great delight; and the mind of at least one of them (if not expressed) was so often impressed with the idea, "What a delightful thing it would be to be a *Missionary.* How nice to *print* these books, and what a privilege to be able to *write* them. Oh, what a happy thing this would be. Men might have all the world for me, if I could but do this. Oh, what a useful art, and what an enviable position—a Minister, who from both pulpit and press, might publish to his poor fellow-sinners the greatness of salvation by so gracious a Saviour."

As this ardent desire, and these feelings, have very much to do with the sequel of this little history, JONATHAN would pause for a moment to urge upon his beloved young readers, not the *crushing* but the *cherishing* of such thoughts, when thus impressed upon the mind, not as a mere passing wish, but as a sober, settled desire after some lawful pursuit. The great object that JONATHAN has in writing this little volume is to encourage his dear young friends in these their lawful and becoming wishes. He would say, Away with the idea that it is an unlikely thing—an impossibility; that it is unreasonable to suppose *you* should ever attain to such and such a position, or that such and such desires are the least likely to be gratified. *In all probability they are to be granted.* The *wish* almost invariably precedes the *realization.* It is in the wise ordainings of PROVIDENCE, that a certain taste for this, that, or the other pursuit, should go before its opening out or accomplishment. And the same God who infuses these desires, when looked up to and acknowledged, does by little and little remove every impediment, and accomplish in and for those who seek Him, "the good pleasure of His will." Even in the common, every-day dispensations of PROVIDENCE, the diligent and persevering man attains his object, if it is a lawful one; how much more those who have grace to wait upon Him, concerning whom Solomon says, "In all thy ways acknowledge Him, and he shall direct thy paths" (Prov. iii. 6). Looking to God, and leaning upon him, JONATHAN would have his dear young friends remember our text—make it their watchword—and, in spite of all difficulties and discouragements,

TRY.

CHAPTER VI.

AN EXAMPLE—JONATHAN'S OLD FRIEND, THE BOOKSELLER—HIS SON—DELICACY AND RESERVE—LOVE FOR STUDY—DESIRE FOR THE MINISTRY—ENTERS COLLEGE—IS ORDAINED—AND BECOMES THE ACCEPTABLE CURATE OF——THE YOUNG COUNTRY PRINTER—GOES TO LONDON—DISAPPOINTMENT—TRIES—INTRODUCED TO A LONDON ESTABLISHMENT—PROGRESSES—PERSEVERES—SELECTED BY HIS EMPLOYER AS HIS SUCCESSOR—COMMENCES BUSINESS—SUCCEEDS — MARRIES —BECOMES A HAPPY HUSBAND, A FOND FATHER, AN INDEPENDENT TRADESMAN.

PERHAPS this may be the best place to give an example of the good resulting from perseverance. JONATHAN called one day upon an old and valued friend, a bookseller, and, after some general conversation, made special inquiries after his family. "They are all well," said he, "and going on very satisfactorily. But there is one," he added, alluding to a tall, delicate young man engaged behind the counter, "that I cannot understand. He is always poring over his Greek Testament, Latin Grammar, or something of the kind. His heart does not seem in the business."

"Indeed," said JONATHAN; "have you any idea where his taste lies?"

"No," was the reply.

"Well, let me TRY him. Perhaps he is a little shy of expressing himself to you, as his father, or to one of his own family."

So saying, JONATHAN presently walked towards him, and began:—

"Well, Theodore, and are you happy at this kind of work?" as he stood sorting and serving sundry kinds of publications.

"Not very, thank you."

"Indeed! Is there anything else you would prefer?"

He was silent; not a word would he speak.

"If your mind," continued JONATHAN, "is set upon anything else, now is the time to say so. You have a kind father, whose delight it would be to do all in his power to further any reasonable request."

Still there was a pause.

"Now let me entreat you to speak, if there is anything pressing upon your mind."

"Well, then," said he, trembling, and with the tear starting to his eye, and a flush to his pallid cheek, "I wish to be in the Church."

"Oh! very good!" was the answer. "Let us TRY what can be done."

"His heart," said JONATHAN, withdrawing from the young man, and once more addressing his father, "is set upon the Ministry."

The father listened with becoming solicitude—with a parent's interest. His children had been well trained. Himself the most persevering and honourable of men, had inculcated in his children, not only habits of industry, but of the utmost self-reliance. Each was in a great measure self-taught, and few families were more remarkable for their sound judgment, good sense, and general information.

"What is to be done?" at length said his father.

"Try St. Bees', or King's College."

Inquiries were promptly made about both the above Universities, which ended in the young man being speedily entered as a student in the latter. He applied himself closely; he *tried* to master every difficulty as one by one they made their appearance; he succeeded to the astonishment of every one. Having completed his College-course, and taken his degree, he next presented himself as a candidate for ordination, having been promised a title by an Incumbent in Lancashire. He passed the Bishop of M———'s examination most creditably; was ordained; and is now, with renovated health, and a zeal becoming that high and holy office to which he has been admitted, fulfilling the arduous duties of the Curacy of ———.

So much for TRYING. This is one instance out of the multitudes that might be quoted. Let one more suffice —a case which is equally well known to JONATHAN. Some years ago, a youth called, in company with his father, upon an extensive London printer. "I have brought my son up from the country," said he, "to place him in a London office; but, not being satisfied with appearances, I have called to ask if you will take him?" The father was so earnest, and the son so anxious, that the employer could not resist the appeal. He had *tried* previously by letter to put the applicant off, by stating what was the fact, that he had no vacancy. But the father being a member of the TRY Company, would not, it seems, be put off; and having, as stated, gone to London, in quest of another situation for his son, called personally upon the party in question—a good example for all who are disposed to TRY, to adopt—and by renewed efforts, succeeded in his object. The youth was received into the establishment. In spite of all the temptations that were thrown in his way, and the many allurements which were presented, by his companions in labour, he kept both heart and hand steadily fixed upon his one object. He made more than ordinary progress; experience was added to merely theoretical knowledge; his employer looked on with satisfaction and pleasure. At length, *his* mind being directed to other pursuits, he proposed to relinquish business. Successorship was offered to this youth—now a young man. For a time he shrank from the responsibility; he pleaded youth and inexperience. He consulted friends, and they discouraged him. But, with a considerable amount of that astonishing stamina, TRY, in him, and falling back upon that noble principle, which, under God, JONATHAN wants to instil into his dear young friends—namely, self-reliance—he at length fell in with the proposal. A certain portion of stock and materials was placed in his hands: his capital in hard cash was but *ten pounds;* he *tried;* he succeeded, that young man is now a devoted husband, a fond father, and a prosperous tradesman.

Inasmuch as most of the parties are still living to whom reference is made in this work, JONATHAN, from feelings of delicacy, is compelled to make but a mere cursory allusion to them. But for this, he might so enlarge upon facts, as to prove yet more fully how advantageous and encouraging is the issue of a steady application. Within his own personal knowledge, JONATHAN has many very striking examples of the most decided success, resulting from a plodding perseverance. Gradually but most effectually have certain small beginnings led on to present high and honourable achievements.

Try, and Try Again.

CHAPTER VII.

ALFRED AND JOHN AGAIN—THE COPPER-PLATE—FIRST ATTEMPT AT PRINTING—WANT OF INK—SUBSTITUTE—IMPRESSION—FAILURE, AND WHY?—COURAGE—DETERMINATION TO TRY AGAIN—INFANT SCHOOL RHYME.

THE young reader will, I am sure, pardon the digression of the last chapter; and I am pleased to think that he will be now anxious to rejoin our two little heroes, Alfred and John. I spoke about their interest in books, and their wish to write and print them. Just about this time, an old name-plate—that is, an old copper-plate, with John's papa's name engraved upon it—came in their way. They thought this a prize indeed, and a good opportunity for *trying* to print; but how was this to be done? The common writing ink was of no use; they could not fill the indentions in the plate with *that,* without staining the surface likewise; and then the impression would be of no service. Their object, therefore, was to make a composition with more substance than the common writing ink, as a mere liquid

was of no use; so at last they got some kind of lamp-black, and, rubbing this into the letters which were cut out on the plate, they then laid a piece of writing paper over all, and, placing a stone upon the plate, left it during school hours. Immediately upon their return from school, they went with no small anxiety to try their success. They raised the stone, and then with the utmost care removed the paper. There were the letters, it was true, but indistinct; there was a want of sharpness and clearness. They were not at the time aware that copper-plate printing-ink must be specially prepared; the plate itself made warm by gas or charcoal; and a much sharper and more powerful pressure brought to bear upon it than their very primitive method of a stone.

However, though their first attempts at printing had no claims to a stall at the London, Dublin, or Paris exhibitions of 1851 and following years, still Alfred and John were not discouraged. They were not so easily beaten. They had no notion of throwing both plate and ink aside, and saying, "It's of no use to TRY." "*I can't*" had no place in their creed. On the contrary, the ideas expressed in the following Infant School Rhyme would best explain their feelings:—

"'Tis a lesson you should heed,
Try, try, try again.
If at first you don't succeed,
Try, try, try again.
Then your courage should appear,
For, if you will persevere,
You will conquer, never fear,
Try, try, try again.

"Once or twice though you should fail,
Try, try, try again.
If you would at last prevail,
Try, try, try again.
If we strive 'tis no disgrace,
Though we may not win the race;
What should you do in that case?
Try, try, try again.

"If you find your case is hard,
Try, try, try again.
Time will bring you your reward,
Try, try, try again.
All that other people do,
Why, with patience, should not you?
Only keep this rule in view,
Try, try, try again."

CHAPTER VIII.

COPPER-PLATE PRINTING TOO HARD FOR BEGINNERS—LETTER-PRESS PREFERABLE—ALFRED'S ERRAND—THE OFFICE WINDOW—FIRST SIGHT OF PRINTING—JOHN AND ALFRED CONFERRING—THEIR ACQUAINTANCE WITH A YOUNG PRINTER—VISIT TO A PRINTING-OFFICE—BOOK-LABELS.

COPPER-PLATE printing was rather a serious beginning for these two juveniles. They might have tried their hand with better success at the letter-press, if so be they had furnished themselves with an alphabet or two of types, a little pad for inking, and a small groove for holding the letters, with a handle for pressing; but at the time of which I speak, Alfred and John knew nothing of such things.

By degrees, however, they came to know more. A little circumstance helped them on their way. It happened that

Alfred was one day sent upon an errand for his father. He had to go into the town in the outskirts of which they lived. In passing through one of the streets he saw an old-fashioned window with small panes of glass, cut diamond-fashion. He thought it strange, and, looking in as he passed, he saw a man and boy engaged just inside the window. First there were two uprights of wood, say three inches thick by six

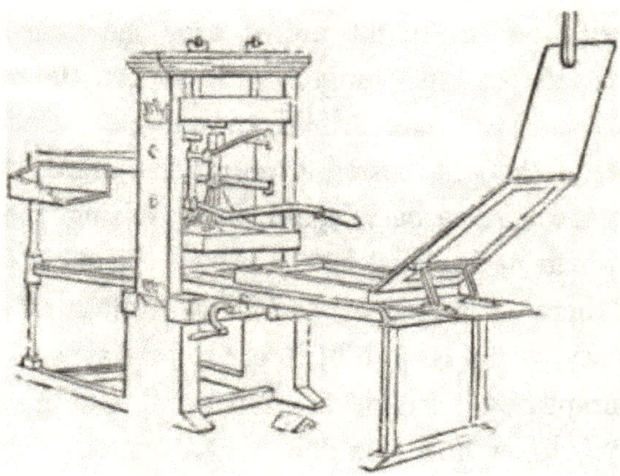

inches broad, and about eight feet high; then there were three or four cross-pieces of about three feet long, which braced the two uprights together; in the centre of two of these cross-pieces was fixed a kind of screw, and attached to this a long handle, which, upon being pulled over, brought down a thick piece of timber, or iron-faced slab, upon a surface of wood, which was made to run in and out upon a sort of tramway.

All this seemed a strange sort of proceeding to Alfred, and at first he could not understand what it meant; but presently he saw a boy step forward from the rear of one of the uprights, and with two large black pallets that he held in his hands, thump away upon something which lay upon the flat surface. In another moment the man placed a blank sheet of paper upon a frame-work to his right hand—turned it down—rolled it under the cross-piece to which the screw was fixed, and then with all his might pulled over the long handle. All this was passing strange. "What can the man and the boy be at?" said Alfred to himself. But almost before the thought passed through his mind, the man turned the surface back again, and, raising the frame upon which he had just before placed the sheet of white paper, there to Alfred's amazement, almost amounting to ecstacy, was a large bill, in clear, bold type! Alfred was enraptured. "This is printing!" said he to himself; "I know how it is done now." And, if he were interested before, he was tenfold more interested now. He waited and waited, and saw the same operation gone through again and again, producing a fresh placard at every turn. Time at last warned him, and reluctantly leaving so pleasant a scene, he ran the rest of the way, to make up for the time thus lost on his errand.

At night Alfred and John had much to talk about, you may be sure. Though the former had got some insight into one part of the process of printing, there were still some difficulties in his mind. What were those types from which the bill was printed, and how were they put together in the form from which they were struck off? Thus Alfred reasoned with himself.

At length by some means he and John became acquainted with a young printer. He was the son of a widow; and, seeing how much these boys were interested in the art in which he was being instructed, he proposed to take the elder to show him the whole process. This was a wonderful treat to Alfred. It was to him about the most charming scene he had ever witnessed. There

was a large room, all round, and in the centre of which, were arranged a number of frames, with a multitude of small compartments, each of which was occupied by a separate letter. Moreover, there were types from the tiniest size to a letter half as big as one's head; and then, unlike the tall wooden frame which he had seen before, there were some three or four modern presses, all iron, and of different sizes and strength.

Soon after this Alfred was taken ill, and John for some days went to school alone. One afternoon, however, a little parcel was placed in Alfred's hand. He opened it, and to his joy what should it contain but his own name printed in full, with that of his beloved companion, as joint librarian? Strange as it may seem, this simple circumstance so roused him, and diverted his mind from his illness, that it proved a more effectual remedy than all the medicine he had taken. He was better from that hour.

CHAPTER IX.

JOHN'S PAPA—LETTERS—LESSONS—ANXIETY FOR HIS BOY—INDIAN BOWS AND ARROWS—THE INDIAN'S SCRUPLES—HORRORS OF WAR.

INTERESTING letters often arrived from John's beloved papa. Not only were they full of interest, but they breathed the language of one whose mind had been blessed by affliction. Under God, they had taught him to build his hopes not upon time, but eternity. He saw that *this* was only the pathway to *that*; that his stay on earth could, at most, be but a few years; and then it might be said of him as of others, "Our fathers, where are they? and the prophets, do they live for ever?" Such had been the intrusion upon his little circle, that he knew full well how true the saying, "What is your life? It is even a vapour that appeareth for a little time, and then vanisheth away." He knew, because he had proved it in his own sad case, that all below the sun is "vanity and vexation of spirit." He had been taught that "this was not his rest, it is polluted."

But he never forgot his boy. Most, if not all his letters, contained one for him, written in a neat, clear hand, and breathing most fervent desires for his welfare. All his human hopes now centred in his loved and only boy. That he might grow up to be a good and useful man, was the one wish of his heart. Sorry indeed am I, that letters which were so carefully preserved, are now not forthcoming, and cannot, consequently, form part of this volume.

One of these letters was one day accompanied by a present, and what do you think it was? Two Indian bows and arrows for Alfred and John. "It was," said Mr. L., "with much difficulty I could procure them. When I asked one Indian to sell me his, he refused, saying, it was his only defence. With the arrows I have sent," continued Mr. L., "I have been at much pains to extract the poison." The bows were about seven feet long, the arrows from three to four; towards the top of the latter, for about ten or twelve inches, the wood was slightly indented in a diamond form, and in these grooves was concealed poison, so that if the arrow should fail to pierce a vital part, it might secure the death of its victim by poison. Never does the ingenuity of man present itself in so painful a light, as when directed to the injury or destruction of his fellow-man. How dreadful is sin in all its aspects.

CHAPTER X.

JOHN'S LOVE FOR LITERATURE, ALFRED'S FOR COMMERCE—JOHN MORE PERSEVERING THAN ALFRED—FOWL-KEEPING—THEIR LOSSES—DANGER OF INSOLVENCY—THE WALK—THE HAIL-STORM—PROSPERITY—REVERSES—THE RESCUED BIRD.

YOUNG as they were, a difference of taste already began to show itself in these two boys. The one was deeply interested in commercial pursuits—the other equally so in literary matters. In the one there was a quickness of thought, but sluggishness of action; in the other, perhaps, less invention and originality, but thorough industry, and the most praiseworthy perseverance.

Of the two, most certainly the latter should be the example. However desirable quick-thoughtedness and keenness of apprehension may be, closeness of application and a determinate perseverance are more to be sought after. This better comports with our motto—TRY. Such was the determination of John, that he has been heard to say, "I have had to read such and such, over and over again, even eight or ten times, before I could catch the meaning, or master it;" whereas, it is not unlikely that Alfred would have laid it aside at a second or third reading, as a hopeless matter.

The different taste of these boys, it has been said,

began to show itself early. Alfred's commercial life commenced in the purchase, wholesale, and vending retail to his schoolfellows, of half-a-gross of lead pencils. With the profits and pocket-money, both Alfred and John set up a poultry-yard, the produce in eggs of which were to be disposed of all the year round at one penny each. But soon after they commenced operations as poulterers, they were likely to have become bankrupts. Their poultry-yard was confined; there was no run for their fowls; more hand-feeding was necessary: barley being dear, and the weather cold, the outlay far exceeded the returns. In fact, the fowls were chilled, and there were no eggs. Our young speculators were in a fright as well as a fix. Upon application to the seller of the fowls, stating that they did not come up to his representations, he said, "Wait till there is a shower of hail, then you may expect some eggs." Taking for granted *he* must know, the patience of our young friends was taxed a little longer: they went on buying and feeding in hope, but still no eggs. At length, one afternoon, having gone with Alfred's venerable father a distance of some two or three miles to walk; upon returning, the hail for which they had so long and anxiously been wishing, came on. The boys' hopes were directly raised; and, begging his father to excuse him, Alfred ran on to see what success in the egg-way. Singular to say, he found an egg in the nest; and, from that time forward, the hens continued to lay. Alfred set it down to the hail; and, being somewhat inflated with their success, he thought to have two eggs a-day from each hen, because he happened to hear one of them cackling, as if for laying.

Unmingled prosperity, however, is not good: so Alfred and John found it. Hence they had very soon to meet another reverse. Either by malice or through accident their live-stock was endangered. One of their hens had its leg broken—this was a sad, sad affair; the two boys were in great grief; but, instead of killing the hen, and selling her carcass, an experiment was tried—Friar's Balsam, and sundry small sticks and bandages.

This happily proved most successful. After a few weeks the hen in question was as strong and as hale as the others.

Again, they had another check. They had been on a visit to some relatives at Plymouth, and, upon starting homewards, were presented with a pair of fowls: they had brought them in safety a distance of 250 miles, and were well pleased with their success, but, as they were letting go the anchor of the ship, one of the passengers gave a shout; the hen had broken out of the basket, and was flying over the side of the steamer, into the sea, when Alfred, attracted by the shout, rushed forward, and happily caught the hen by the leg, just as she was flying over the gunwale.

CHAPTER XI.

JOHN'S TASTE FOR LEARNING—IMPATIENCE AT PLAY—HIS FIRST ATTEMPT AT BLANK VERSE—THE GRAMMAR-SCHOOL—EARLY RELIGIOUS IMPRESSIONS—THE DARK ROOM—FORTITUDE—THE FOLLY OF FEAR.

JOHN, after all, was little more than what tradesmen call a "sleeping partner" in the poultry concern. He was more for books than business. Nay, he became so bent upon the attainment of knowledge, that he now frequently had not the patience to stay and play out a game, but would actually on a sudden run away, and leave Alfred in the lurch. This was anything but pleasant to the latter. But John had the benefit of it in after-days; he was well repaid for all his pains. He was scarcely twelve years of age, when he wrote a piece of blank verse of some hundred and fifty lines, which, without his knowledge, the editor of a highly respectable provincial journal readily accepted for insertion. Soon after this, John was placed at a grammar-school, as introductory to a University course. The tenor of his mind at this time may be seen by one or two circumstances which are worth mentioning. His grandmamma had, on one occasion, been praying with her family, as she was wont to do, when, upon rising from their knees, John modestly said to her, "Grandmamma, you prayed that we might be the made monuments of God's sparing mercy. We *are* that. Should you not rather have prayed that we may be made the subjects of His saving grace?" Again, after a sermon, he was commonly prepared to give a clear and intelligent account of it. His tone of mind, and superiority over his companion, might also be seen by other facts. When very young, and before John's family circle was broken up, he and Alfred happened to be sleeping in a dark room. The latter, though the elder, was alarmed, and roused the family, whilst John in vain, with the utmost calmness, sought to quiet him, and pacify his fears. Again, at a somewhat later date, upon the death of an uncle, Alfred's eldest sister took John by the hand to show the corpse. John walked calmly up to the couch, whilst Alfred barely entered the room, and stood trembling at the foot. The moment the face was uncovered, though John stood composedly by, Alfred made a dart out of the house to his home, in the greatest possible terror.

Moreover, at a still later day, and when both Alfred and John were arrived at years of maturity, the former had been summoned home by the sudden death of a beloved sister. So speedy was her illness and death, that decomposition instantly setting in, Alfred was not allowed to see her; but, previous, to his arrival, of his own accord John had gone several times, in the stillness of the night, to the room where she was lying, to gaze upon her sacred remains.

Dear boys, there are those who are martyrs to fear where no fear in reality is. How desirable, then, the seeking after and the cultivation of a steady fixedness of mind and purpose. Bravado, or a careless defiance of danger, is one thing; but a calm consideration of difficulty, and corresponding resolve to meet it, quite another; the one is to be avoided, the other cherished. And, in a youth's after-course in life, how much good, under God, will accrue from the exercise of thought, watchfulness, and care.

CHAPTER XII.

JOHN AS AN ORPHAN—PROMPTINGS TO PERSEVERANCE—HIS FORETHOUGHT—"PREVENTION BETTER THAN CURE"—ALFRED MORE HEEDLESS, AND, IN CONSEQUENCE, THE GREATER SUFFERER—A CAUTION—JOHN BENEFITED BY OTHERS' TRIALS—ALFRED IN NEED OF AN ADVISER.

PERHAPS the fact of John being left an orphan had much to do with the formation of his character. Notwithstanding the kindness of friends—and that was unbounded—there is no doubt that the recollection of his dependent position would oftentimes present itself to John's mind, and prompt him to exertion. It is equally probable that it begat thoughtfulness and prudence.

It was often said within hearing of these youths, "the young especially should *think* before they *speak;*" certain it is that, in John's case, he would ever "*think* before he *acted.*" He would carefully weigh the matter, and learn to view it in all its bearings; and thus a flaw might be remedied here, and a failure avoided there, which but for this forethought might have followed. On the contrary, Alfred was more the creature of *impulse*. He scarcely gave himself time to *think*, but *acted* for most part on the spur of the moment. He might almost be said to *act* first, and *think* after. Hence through life Alfred met with many a bitter disappointment, and was the subject of pain and regret, which a little more foresight might have avoided. It has been said that Alfred suffered tenfold more than John, and to this simple cause very much of his sorrow might be ascribed. Dear young readers, try to think of this. May this little work have this happy tendency upon your minds. Forget not, as you read, that it is plain matter of fact which is here brought before you.

Fond as both these youths were of reading, there is not a question that the one turned what he read to much better account than the other. John gained by *others' experience*, whilst Alfred had to *learn for himself*. Hence his frequent pain and anguish. Alfred thus stood in need continually of a kind, judicious adviser, whilst John was one, for most part, to himself. It is not improbable that it would have been of immense advantage, could these youths have journeyed through life together; their course, however, was destined to be, at least for a time, totally different. They walked in close and endearing companionship up to a certain point, and then their after-course was in very opposite directions. Contemplating these youths as they went hand in hand, and heart bound about heart, it could scarcely have been supposed that their future pursuits would have been so unlike.

CHAPTER XIII.

THE MOURNING LETTER—JOHN'S FATHER DIES IN JAMAICA OF YELLOW FEVER—THE DEATH-BED SCENE—HIS DIARY—ANXIETY FOR HIS FAR-DISTANT BOY—THE FAMILY REGISTER—THE INTERLEAVED BIBLE—A VOICE FROM THE TOMB.

I SPOKE in my last chapter of John being left an orphan. The reader will remember it was in consequence of the death of his dear mamma, and afterwards of his brother and sister, that he and Alfred became so closely united. After so great a loss, however, he still had one left, and, though but one, yet in him centred all that was kind, affectionate, and tender. But there was another affliction in reserve for John. The post one morning brought a letter as usual, but it was written in another hand, and its black border and seal bespoke additional pain. The letter in question was opened by John's beloved grandpapa, and in it was found the mournful tidings that John's dear father was no more! Whilst residing at Kingston, in Jamaica, and just after he had spent a delightful evening with some Christian

friends, he returned home—was seized with yellow fever, which, in the short space of three or four days, ended his valuable life!

Apart from that Christian circle in the midst of which he moved, and by whom he was so highly and deservedly esteemed, it was painful to think of him as languishing upon the bed of pain, so far away from his own immediate kindred and friends. How vivid to his recollection must have been that former death-bed, the first indication of the breaking-up of his own loved circle. Truly he might have felt—and his own diary and letters seemed to imply it—that he was speedily to rejoin one whom on earth he had loved so well. It was his doubtless to rejoice in the fact, that in that better land upon which he was about to enter, there should be no more death, nor sorrow, nor sin; that there God would wipe away tears from their eyes; and that former scenes o. suffering should in very deed have for ever passed away. But there was one, notwithstanding, for whom he was willing to linger even in this vale of sorrow. There was one on whose account he would have cheerfully consented to postpone his bliss. There was one whom he would have loved personally to have "trained up in the way he should go, so that when he was old he might not depart from it." But that loved one—his own darling boy—was far, far away; too far—if not indeed too young—to soothe a father's dying pillow; too remote to bathe those throbbing temples, and to moisten the parched lips. But, in the interval of consciousness, his loved boy was upon his heart; and his name and claim put before the God and Father of all his mercies, with an intensity of fervour and devotion. His dying words, wrote a friend, were on behalf of his loved but far-distant boy; that God might guard and guide him here, make him useful—and, at last, receive him into His own everlasting embrace.

I have before me at this moment his family Bible; and, in the register which is prefixed, I find inserted in his own handwriting the following :—

"Louisa, the wife of Richard D. Lane, and mother of the above three children, died on Tuesday morning at 12 o'clock, 25th November, 1817, of a consumption, after a lingering illness of eight months, which she was enabled to bear with Christian patience and resignation; aged 27 years and six months. In her walk through life, and in her death, she left a blessed testimony to the truth as it is in Christ Jesus. Her last words were, that her hope was founded alone on the blood and righteousness of Jesus.

"In her, her afflicted family has lost an affectionate wife—a dutiful daughter—a tender mother—a kind sister—and a sincere friend.

"She looked well to the ways of her household, and ate not the bread of idleness. Her children shall rise up and call her blessed: her husband also, and he praiseth her. Many daughters hath done virtuously, but she excelleth them all."

In the same register, in the handwriting of dear John himself, after the record of the death of his youthful brother and infant sister, is that of the death of his beloved papa, as expressed in the following terms :—

"Richard Dickenson Lane, Sen., died at Kingston, Jamaica, of the yellow fever, May 5th, 1819, and was buried in the English burial-ground at that place.

"'As we believe that Jesus died and rose again, even so them that sleep in Jesus will God bring with him' (1 Thess. iv. 14.)"

Thus it will appear that Mr. Lane did not outlive his beloved wife two years, and during the interval, two of his three children having died, John was bereft of all within that short period.

Upon the arrival in England of Mr. Lane's books and clothes after his decease, a Bible, which seemed to have been his own special reading-bible, was given to Alfred. And the state of his mind might have been traced by the particular marks and underlinings which it contained. They had evidently afforded the deceased great comfort. The corner of nearly every leaf was turned down, pointing to some special verse or line. The 28th Psalm was braced, and under it was written, "Graciously given in answer to prayer, 23rd March, 1819." This was but little more than a month before he died. Will the reader turn to it, and see how suitable such a portion for one in Mr. Lane's circumstances, bereft and destitute, on the one hand; and, though at the time ignorant of the fact, upon the very threshold of an eternal world, on the other?

Oh, that my dear young readers may, through the same sovereign mercy, be enabled to say, "The Lord is *my* strength and *my* shield: my heart trusted in Him, and I am helped: therefore my heart greatly rejoiceth, and with my song will I praise Him."

Ere this little book is closed we shall see how far Mr. Lane's hopes and expectations were fulfilled in reference to his son. That they were confirmed in his own case, there was also abundant proof. He left among his papers a diary rich in Christian knowledge and experience; his last entry in which was made only three or four days before his death.

As a key to the state of his mind, and his own personal knowledge of the things of God, it may be mentioned, that the corners of sundry leaves of his Bible were directed to these portions: "And they that know Thy name will put their trust in Thee" (Psal. ix. 10); "O fear the Lord, ye His saints; for there is no want to them that fear Him" (Psal. xxxiv. 9); "O God, thou hast taught me from my youth: and hitherto have I declared Thy wondrous works" (Psalm lxxi. 17); "Nevertheless I am continually with Thee: Thou hast holden me by my right hand" (Psal. lxxiii. 23); "Thou hast forgiven the iniquity of Thy people, Thou hast covered all their sin" (Psal. lxxxv. 2); "Nor for the pestilence that walketh in darkness; nor for the destruction that wasteth at noonday" (Psal. cxi. 9); "Remember me, O Lord, with the favour that Thou bearest unto Thy people: O visit me with Thy salvation" (Psal. cvi. 4); "This is the Lord's doing; it is marvellous in our eyes" (Psal. cxviii. 23).

Again, the last chapter of the Book of Ecclesiastes, as well as many portions in the early part of the Book of Proverbs, were specially turned down; and is it not more than likely that as he read that Divine injunction, "Remember now thy Creator in the days of thy youth, while the evil days come not, nor the years draw nigh, when thou shalt say, I have no pleasure in them;" his heart went up in fervent breathings to the Lord, that his own dear but far distant boy might have grace to "remember *his* Creator in the days of his youth?"

Dear, dear youthful reader, as "he being dead, yet speaketh," may you have grace to hear; may the simple marks in that precious Bible prove to be as so many finger-posts in Divine Providence to your consciences, effectually calling upon you, "so to number your days, that you may apply your hearts unto wisdom;" that you may learn the answer to the all-important question, "Wherewithal shall a young man cleanse his way?" namely, "by taking heed thereto, *according to Thy word.*"

CHAPTER XIV.

JOHN STILL AT SCHOOL—ALFRED LEAVES HOME—PARENTAL ADMONITION—HOME-PANGS—THE LONELY WALK—THE PRIVILEGES OF HOME—JONATHAN'S RECOLLECTIONS—REGRETS—PARENTS TO BE LOVED AND CHERISHED.

NOW we must return to John and Alfred themselves. The former, we have said, was placed at a grammar-school; the latter's mind being set upon commercial pursuits, was placed on trial in a printing-office some twenty miles away. This of necessity led to a separation; and bitter moments they were when John and Alfred parted upon yonder shore, and when Alfred (just turned thirteen years of age) first quitted the parental roof. It was a trial, and solemn were the words of his beloved parents:

"You are going to leave home," said they, "and you will meet with many temptations; but remember we are clear of your blood." This pierced like an arrow to Alfred's heart; he was young, and sanguine too; and his ardent desire to learn the art upon which his mind had been so long and so devotedly fixed, bore him up; but he little thought of all that a boy's leaving his own dear home entailed. He never left home so cheerfully afterwards. It was a novelty then; but, as that novelty wore away, it became harder and harder every time to tear himself away from the embraces of those he so tenderly loved. On one occasion, some three or four years after this, he had left home in the morning, and had reached his destination; but his home-pangs overpowered him; and he turned round, and set out upon his return journey of twenty long miles. When scarcely a third of the distance, night set in. He found himself on the borders of a dark bleak common, over which there were various paths leading to very different places. He felt his desolation, and the liability of losing his way. He knelt down upon that barren heath; and, putting his trembling hands together, prayed the Lord to take care of him, and to guide him aright. He rose—walked on —and reached his home just after midnight.

Ah, dear young people, what a mercy it is, in times of separation from friends, or in seasons of heart-sorrow, loneliness, and desolation, to know and feel that there is One always at hand, and always able and willing to hear. Do you not remember the story of Jacob, and of his leaving his home? What a dreary journey his!- how solitary his lot that night when, wearied and sad, and because "the sun was set, he took of the stones of that place, and put them for his pillows, and lay down in that place to sleep." Little did he then think who was so near to him—who was condescending to watch over and to preserve him. Hence when he awoke, after his eventful dream, he exclaimed, "Surely, the Lord is in

this place, and I knew it not. And he was afraid, and said, How dreadful is this place! this is none other than the house of God, and this is the gate of heaven." "And Jacob vowed a vow, saying, "If God will be with me, and will keep me in this way that I go, and will give me bread to eat, and raiment to put on, so that I come again to my father's house in peace; then shall the

Lord be my God: and this stone, which I have set for a pillar, shall be God's house: and of all that thou shalt give me I will surely give the tenth unto thee." Jacob always afterwards loved to think of and occasionally to visit Bethel. It was a place very dear to his remembrance. It was where he may be said to have set out for heaven. He there commenced, as it were, a double journey—that of this life, and that of the life to come! It proved, indeed, to him to be the very "gate of heaven." And, though Jacob had plenty of trouble after that, yet he had always the God of Bethel to go to. The patriarch proved, as did the Psalmist, that "when his father and his mother forsook him, then the Lord would take him up." So that when Jacob drew near to the end of his days, and was about to bless the two sons of his long-lost but now restored Joseph, he said, "God, before whom my fathers, Abraham, and Isaac, did walk, the God which fed me all my life long unto this day; the angel which redeemed me from all evil, bless the lads."

Oh, dear young reader, be it your mercy to seek and to find the self-same God; for, though Jacob is dead, and prophets, apostles, and martyrs, yet the God of Abraham, Isaac, and Jacob still lives; still He sits upon the throne of grace "waiting to be gracious;" and still His language is, "I love them that love me, and those that seek me early shall find me."

Moreover, may the dear youth whose eyes now run over these lines learn to value more and more the privileges, the blessings, all the fond endearments of home! Nothing (humanly speaking) can make amends for home! It is

> "Home, sweet, sweet home!
> Be it ever so humble,
> There's no place like home!"

Parents! dear parents! oh the privilege! How does JONATHAN's heart bleed over the memory of long-gone parents; and even now, old as he is, the thought will occasionally arise, "Oh, what a boon to have one hour's converse with the dear departed ones." Though he was deemed, for most part, an obedient boy, yet, even at this distant day, there are recollections of selfishness and a want of a more becoming consideration, that deeply, deeply wound him; so that JONATHAN sighs over the language as somewhere expressed—

> "I grew up selfish, full of thoughts and cares
> For my own good, but unconcerned for theirs:
> I gave cold service; but the smile that cheers,
> The softer tone that soothes declining years,
> These I withheld; they felt it,
> And the dart that wounded them
> Now rankles in my heart.
> They had their failings; ah, dear parents,
> How those few infirmities have vanished now!"

Yea, twenty years and more have rolled away since JONATHAN betrayed a little impatience when his loved mother was seeking at a certain terrace a friend. Not succeeding at this or that door, she persevered; she tried; JONATHAN was fidgetty—impatient; that loved one looked—she spoke not—but oh that look so full of love, and tenderness, and pity—it has pierced OLD JONATHAN to the heart a thousand and a thousand times since; and he has thought again and again of the scene pictured to him in early days—the little girl with tearful eye bending over her mother's grave in the village churchyard, exclaiming—

"Ah, if she would but come again,
I think I'd vex her so no more."

Dear young friends, take an affectionate warning word from one now passing the downhill of life—who was once a son, and has now long been a father—be watchful, tender, courteous to them who will be *yours* but a very few years at most. Oh, learn to think and feel for them before you think and feel for yourselves. Give them, next to God, the *first place;* the other will follow as a matter of course. Nor will you be losers thereby, but immense gainers. You will enjoy by such a course a satisfaction, pleasure, and joy, which nothing earthly can afford.

CHAPTER XV.

ALFRED'S FIRST VOYAGE—THE DEBTORS' WARD—WANTS TO GIVE HIS MONEY—ENTERS A PRINTING-OFFICE—PROGRESSES—HIS FELLOW-APPRENTICE—MASTER'S SON A YOUNG TYRANT—THE DAILY CROSS—A DINNER-SCENE—ALFRED'S REMOVAL.

AN elder brother took charge of Alfred on his way to the town where he was about to be located. At that time steam-vessels were scarcely known. Sailing smacks, as they were called, used to ply between the ports; and on board one of these Alfred's brother and himself took their passage. Some three hours brought them to their destination. The first building they passed after they landed was a prison or debtor's ward, from the grated window of which, tied to a pole, was a tin box, with the words, "Please to remember the poor debtors," painted on it. Alfred's first impression was to put at least a part (if not the whole) of his little pocket-money into this box, for he thought it such a sad thing for these poor prisoners to be pent up there. This his

first essay had to be gently checked by his more prudent brother, as doubtless he foresaw such a course, followed out without thought or consideration, would soon ensure for Alfred himself the poor debtor's fate. It was an early lesson certainly, and perhaps was a pretty plain proof of how much he had to learn.

Alfred's progress in printing was most rapid. His heart was so set upon it, and he was so resolved to TRY, that he "learnt the cases"—that is, the roundabout position of the alphabet in its different compartments

—in little more than an hour. He then soon learnt to "compose"—that is, to arrange the types, one by one, and line after line, in the "composing-stick." Then the "imposing," which is to place the types so composed in an iron frame, and transfer them from a flat stone or iron surface to the press, where a proof-sheet having been taken—read by the author's copy, and corrected (should there prove to be any mistakes), the given number of copies is then struck off at the press, and the type distributed, or put back into its varied compartments, to be re-set or composed in another form.

Alfred was little less than enchanted with his new occupation. He gave his mind to it. He steadily, perseveringly applied himself. Hence he speedily overcame every difficulty; and in a few months outdid a fellow-apprentice, who, for want of interest, had spent nearly seven years to little purpose.

But, though Alfred had a kind master, his patience was about to be put to a very severe test. Soon after the elder apprentice had completed his term, the employer's son was taken into the printing-office. He being the only boy, was petted and humoured by his mother. He became, in consequence, a disobedient, self-willed boy. Alfred soon saw how matters were; for he had not long been an inmate of the house, ere this boy made an attack upon him. Alfred resisted, and, being the bigger of the two, got the mastery. For this he received a severe lecture from his master's wife. He then foresaw he must take his choice of two evils, namely, either to submit to the boy in question, or render his temporary home uncomfortable by constant disputes with the mistress. Of the two evils, he thought the former the least; and what he endured in consequence was beyond expression. For a length of time, without naming it to a creature, he suffered a very martyrdom. The boy was a perfect tyrant. Every annoyance that he met with from other quarters, he vented upon Alfred; and the more patiently the latter bore it, the worse the former seemed. At length matters came to a crisis. That wicked boy began, as usual, to irritate, in order to raise a quarrel; and then, seizing a heavy broom-stick, actually broke it in two across Alfred's arm. How it was the arm itself was not fractured was astonishing. This, however, was too much for Alfred. He could bear it no longer; and, with one blow, he felled his persecutor to the ground. But the moment he had done so, his heart relented; he ran, raised him, and set him upon his knee, whilst the stricken youth vowed he would have his revenge.

Thus matters went on for some three years; and it seemed at times as though there would never be an end. But God ordered it for the best. It proved to be one means of teaching Alfred the vanity of all things here. It served to open up much of the wickedness of the human heart, both in himself and others. It checked his natural buoyancy, which might have run him into the most ruinous excesses, now that he was no longer under a parent's eye; and, together with the tender watchings of an elder brother, was one among other means of leading him to the footstool of mercy, in quest of the forgiveness of his sins, and that adoption whereby he might be privileged to cry, Abba, Father. Many a smile, therefore, from the God of the whole earth, was that hapless youth the means of procuring for him he so persecuted. I say hapless, for his career was a lamentable one. He went from bad to worse, though he had warning upon warning.

On one occasion a part of the family were sitting at the dinner-table. As was oftentimes the case, this youth raised a dispute with an elder sister, and, to establish his point, blasphemously wished what he was eating might choke him, or be his death, if it were not true. He had scarcely said the words, ere what he was eating, lodging in his throat, he sprang from the table, and rushed from the room in a state of suffocation. His face turned black, and he was almost gone. It was a distressing scene. But, instead of its humbling him, the moment he recovered he renewed his abuse.

Through God's sovereign grace and mercy, Alfred had now learnt to pray. He had found in God a Father and a Friend indeed; and at times he would beseech the Lord to remove him to a more congenial sphere; to place him where he might find a kindred spirit: for how differently was he circumstanced now to the time when he had enjoyed the close companionship of his beloved John.

At length, and in the most remarkable and unexpected

way, the Lord answered his prayer. He took him from that persecuting youth; but, strange as it may appear, instead of placing him among God-fearing persons, he had now to take a situation in the midst of a number of blasphemers. He had not now *one* persecutor merely, but several who sought day by day to entangle and to injure him. The malice of one rose one day to such a height that he tried to strangle Alfred. He was a tall, powerful man; and, seizing him by the throat, he thrust him up into a corner, and how Alfred escaped was marvellous. But in that, as well as in a variety of other instances, he saw most clearly the preserving and delivering hand of his God; and, even in those early days, was permitted to learn his first lessons out of the promise, "No weapon formed against thee shall prosper; and every tongue rising in judgment against thee thou shalt condemn."

CHAPTER XVI.

CONSEQUENCES OF DISOBEDIENCE — THE WIDOWED MOTHER — HER DEATH — THE SAD DEATH OF A BLASPHEMER — SICKNESS AND DEATH OF A GAY YOUNG WORLDLING.

HE young reader may want to know what became of Alfred's opponents. The first may truly be said to have "brought down the grey hairs of his parents with sorrow to the grave." Some eighteen months after he had left, his first master died; and, as Alfred stood by his coffin, gazing upon his wasted frame, his widow said, "I do not mean to say that your leaving was the direct cause of his death; but he was never the same afterwards. I said to him one day, 'Why, how is it you do not take the interest in the printing-office that you used to do?' 'Because,' said he (speaking of his son), 'he is so perverse, whilst Alfred and I were so comfortable together.'" The son, after his father's death, continued a wild and most profligate career. His poor widowed mother had long discovered her mistake, and felt the sad effects of her unwise indulgence. Her son became a constant source of *dread*. She would wait his return home, at all hours, night after night, in a pitiable state of suspense and mental pain. At length she died; and her son's business having come to nought, the last Alfred saw of him was just after he had been liberated from prison, to which he had been committed upon some political offence.

The tall man before spoken of died in a poor-house, quite insane. He was a fearful blasphemer; and, in his proud defiance of religion, would sometimes say to Alfred, "If you are within fifty miles of me when I die, I will send for you, that you may see how I die." Poor man! he little thought how near it was, and how sad his end would be.

Another, in the same establishment, equally opposed to religion—a blasphemer, and given up to every species of what the world calls pleasure, was one day suddenly taken ill. His mind had been set upon going to a certain ball which was about to be given; but, a press of business preventing, he was so disappointed that he was compelled to withdraw from the printing-office and take to his bed. In a few days, from a stout hale young man, he had fallen away to a comparative shadow. He left his bed—walked round the office; and, as though doubting his return, took leave of each of his former companions, went home, and shortly after died.

CHAPTER XVII.

THE USE OF TRIAL—TENDS TO WATCHFULNESS AND PRAYER—THE ELECTION — SUNDAY EMPLOYMENT — CONSCIENTIOUS SCRUPLES — THEIR TRIUMPH.

WHETHER Alfred was right in keeping his trial to himself, in reference to his master's son, is a question. He had just cause for complaint; and, perhaps, by clearly stating his case, matters might have somewhat improved. But be this as it may, there is not a doubt that the trial was of great service. It has been said how unwary he was—how prone to be thrown off his guard, and liable to be led into evil. He had just reached a most critical age; and God, in His great mercy, so wrought, that first the tyrannical youth, and, after him, those sundry persecuting young men, should almost of necessity lead him to keep watch over both his tongue and his steps. He knew that they were always on the alert, striving to catch him in his words, and seeking occasion against him. Though painful to bear, this was a blessing in disguise. It led him to pray. He had to ask, day by day, for wisdom, and grace, and strength; and, times without number, he saw that "God was on his side," and that he had no real cause "to fear what man might do unto him."

Two facts will help to show this. For a few weeks during a general election, there was an excess of business. Not only were the hands employed the greater part of several nights, but also three or four Sabbaths in succession. The employer was an ungodly man, and despised religion to the utmost. Alfred expected orders to come on the Sunday, the same as others; but this he was resolved to refuse. He had said he would remain till midnight on the Saturday, and return after midnight on the Sunday, but upon *its* sacred hours he would on no account trespass. Rather than do this, he would resign his situation. Strange to say, *he* was made an exception; he was never asked to attend the office on the Sabbath.

This, as a matter of course, excited the jealousy of his persecutors, and made them still more angry. They became yet more vigilant, in order to detect some flaw in his conduct, and thus to injure him. A plot was laid, that a dispute might follow. In the midst of the dispute, the employer was called. His own brother was the principal actor in the affair. A strict scrutiny was made, and the decision was given against him. He was to pay a fine, or leave. This he refused to do. At this crisis, Alfred saw his employer, and said, "I will not be the means of separating brothers, and therefore I resign my situation." "It is very laudable on your part," was the reply; "but I will not accept it. My brother was in the wrong; and, if he will not conform, the rules of my establishment shall not be infringed on his account."

Some time after this, one evening the employer sent for Alfred, and said, "To-morrow, at eleven o'clock, I purpose discharging every person in my employ, except yourself and one other person." "I thank you, sir," said Alfred, "for this mark of confidence; but, since you have sent for me in this friendly manner, permit me to urge you to pause before you take such a step. It is a very important one, and involves much risk. Some of those you propose to discharge have been with you for many years, whilst the person on whose account you have come to this decision has scarcely been known to you as many months. It is possible you may be deceived in him." The next day came, and the given hour; but no discharge: and, strange to say, the individual in question soon after left the establishment, and became a most formidable rival.

JONATHAN has dwelt upon these facts somewhat at large, in order to convince his young readers that *truth* and *straitforwardness,* however they may be tested and opposed, will, in the end, bring their own reward.

Men of the world, however opposed to godliness, and though they may say and do hard things, know at the same time in whom to confide, and from what sources to expect the strictest honour and integrity. There is not the slightest cause to sacrifice principle, or to compromise character: it is the *plain, honest, direct course* which will ever be found to be the best.

JONATHAN ardently desires that his dear young friends may be blessed with that upright, straightforward principle that will enable them to meet their fellows, not with the shrinking, downcast look, but that manly—at the same time modest—bearing which carries truthfulness and conviction with it, and must of necessity commend itself. Most strongly JONATHAN would urge upon his young friends to avoid everything like depth, double-dealing, equivocation, or the not meeting any question or circumstance in a fair, plain, above-board manner. *Should you have done wrong, say so at once.* Do not hide or cloak it, and thus make matters worse. This will destroy confidence—the other promote it. And, since there is so little honesty in the world, its rarity will cause the injured one to forgive and forget the fault, in his admiration of the sound principles of the offender. Shifting, equivocation, and lying are so pitiful; whilst frankness and candour are to be commended.

CHAPTER XVIII.

EARLY AFFECTIONS—GOD TO BE ACKNOWLEDGED—IMPROBABILITIES—THE STREETS OF LONDON—ALFRED AND HIS COMPANION—THE LARGE BUILDING—SINGULAR COINCIDENCE—ENCOURAGEMENT TO "TRY."

FOR months and even years another train of circumstances proved a very severe test and trial to Alfred. His position was one of extreme suffering. It was of necessity one in which no creature could help. The tenderest feelings of the heart were touched, without, for a season, any response or sympathy. This was another voice in Divine Providence—another invitation from Him who hath said, "Call upon me in the day of trouble, I will deliver thee, and thou shalt glorify me." God was, in consequence, sought. To His footstool Alfred went, morning, noon, and night, for wisdom, strength, submission, courage.

At the throne of grace, he could pour out his heart as into the bosom of a kind and devoted Friend. Patience was what he craved; acquiescence too; and an eye to watch, and a heart to feel, the gracious Providence of God. He felt he had nothing to look to in himself. He dared not trust to even the best of human fathers. He knew what uncertainty cleaved to everything earthly. He saw "it was not in man that walketh to direct his steps." God only could guard and guide him. His, and His alone, were "the cattle upon a thousand hills," and the gold and silver also. True, a thousand difficulties would present themselves. The furtherance of Alfred's wishes seemed out of the question. Much depression was oftentimes the consequence. Still, when waiting upon God, he was cheered, and helped to ask for grace to try and wait His will, and the gracious openings of Providence. "Is there anything too hard for the Lord?" was to him a cheering thought. And, though his patience was taxed, yet God, in His own good time, did, in the most signal and loving way, appear, removing every obstacle, clearing His young disciple's way, and giving him abundant cause to acknowledge and admire Jehovah's wisdom, mercy, grace, and strength.

It was at a period somewhat earlier in his history than that now under consideration—when only about fifteen years of age—he was on a visit to some relatives in London. He was walking one day with a beloved cousin through a certain street, when happening to see a huge building in the distance, he said, "George, what a splendid printing-office that would make." Strange to say, though he was only then a youth serving his apprenticeship upwards of eighty miles away—the building itself occupied, and devoted to a totally different use—yet, a long time afterwards, that very

youth rented those self-same premises, and carried on the printing there on a large scale, for many years. What to all appearance was more improbable? After this, where is the youth who would refuse to

TRY?

CHAPTER XIX.

JOHN'S PROGRESS AT THE GRAMMAR-SCHOOL—PRIZE—ENTERS CAMBRIDGE—FATHERLY COUNSEL AS TO CHOICE OF COMPANIONS—THE TEMPTATIONS OF A UNIVERSITY—JOHN'S PRINCIPLES—HIS ABSTAINING FROM ALL APPEARANCE OF EVIL—HIS COLLEGE ASSOCIATES AND THEIR DEVOTIONAL MEETINGS.

DOUBTLESS my young readers would now be glad to hear something more of John. We left him, as you will remember, at a grammar-school, in close pursuit of his studies. After each examination, John returned home with a prize.

At length he was entered at Cambridge. The husband of the aunt referred to in an earlier chapter took a most lively interest in his welfare. He accompanied him to Cambridge, and, having entered him at St. John's, left him with the best and most parental advice as to what should be his mode of procedure in a position exposed to temptations of no ordinary character.

He would meet with taunts on the one hand, allurements on the other; pretended friendships here, and crafty conspiracies there; this so pleasant, that so harmless: all combined, would render his position most perplexing, and cause him to need, equally with his former companion, special grace to repel temptation in its varied forms and attractions. Both John and Alfred were now very differently circumstanced, yet each stood in need of that wisdom and strength which cometh down from above. But, apart from every other consideration, John was much more adapted for Cambridge trials and temptations than Alfred; and herein was the mercy of God shown. Alfred's was not the mind to grapple with scenes against which John's would present the boldest front. There was too much *easy compliance* with Alfred for a Cambridge career. Without special grace, his disposition would have been sure to have betrayed him. The marvel was that he escaped as he did in his own position. It was to God alone that escape was to be ascribed. He stood repeatedly upon a vortex. Snares were laid for his feet, in which he was wellnigh taken again and again; and, had he been so taken, ruin must have been the result. But, as was said in an earlier page, John was blessed with grace and strength of mind to shun the very "appearance of evil." There was no parleying with *him*—no trifling with temptation; but his steady purpose, fixed principles, and holy determination, helped him, by God's grace, to adopt a course, and to follow it out, that saved him much bitterness of heart and keenness of sorrow. True it is he had, as remarked in a former chapter, a hasty, passionate temper; but he knew it; and his consciousness of that infirmity led him the more carefully to watch over his spirit, lest it should betray him into conduct or language unbecoming his position. His conscience was exceedingly tender, and the language of his heart unceasingly, "Keep back Thy servant from presumptuous sins."

Happily, in most respects, he was enabled to form connexions in his college, where, apart from the frivolity and dissipation which prevailed around, he met with kindred spirits. They had their devotional meetings, and strengthened each others' hearts and hands. Some of those, after fulfilling the engagements of a high and responsible calling as missionaries, have since gone to their great account.

CHAPTER XX.

A FIXED OBJECT THE FORERUNNER OF SUCCESS—THE EVIL OF A WAVERING, UNSETTLED MIND—JOHN'S RESOLUTION—HIS PROGRESS AT CAMBRIDGE—OBTAINS A FELLOWSHIP—SICK CHAMBERS OF IMMENSE PRACTICAL ADVANTAGE TO THE MINISTRY—THE DYING AUNT—JOHN'S RECORD.

I SAID that, under God, few have their minds steadily fixed upon the attainment of a certain laudable object, who do not attain that object. As the laying of a good foundation is to all but half-build the house, so the subject well weighed, and the mind steadily fixed, the end is almost sure of attainment. It is the hesitating, the wavering, the being tossed hither and thither without any distinct purpose, that ends in defeat. "He that wavereth," says the apostle James, "is like a wave of the sea, driven with the wind and tossed." "A double-minded man," says the same apostle, "is unstable in all his ways." Hence a cool determination—a settled resolution to TRY—accomplishes so much.

It was upon this principle John so well succeeded. His mind had long been set upon Cambridge; he paved the way to it by the most determined perseverance; he attained his desire, but that attainment was, in one sense, only to place him upon the threshold of the good he sought. It was but another starting-place—the entrance upon a course where new difficulties and fresh dangers were to beset his path. But he persevered—he *tried*—he succeeded. Term after term placed him higher—higher still. He came off at his examination with the greatest credit; insomuch that towards or at the close of his college course, his fellowship and tutorship produced him nearly £800 a-year.

But the amassing of mere money was never John's object. He thought little of it. He was generous to a degree; and gratitude was a most pleasing trait in his character. When that beloved friend who had been the principal means of placing him at Cambridge was removed by death, he, in turn, became the devoted friend of the widow and the fatherless. They all resided under the same roof at Cambridge; and at the death-bed of that bereaved one (their early and devoted friend and instructress) John and Alfred met. Most touching was that scene; and, equally so, when afterwards they stood together at her grave.

Sick chambers and dying beds—though distasteful to

the worldly, the thoughtless, and the gay—are the loved resort of the Bible student, and furnish practical and profitable materials for the pulpit. John, in these circumstances, was under training for a high and holy service. The following are brief extracts from his journal, kept in relation to scenes which he was then called to witness:—

Feb. 29, 1837.—To me my dearest aunt said, "God bless you, my dear John; follow hard after Him;" and at another time on the same day, urged me to follow on. To W.* she said, "'Wherewithal shall a young man cleanse his way? even by taking heed thereto according to Thy word.' You will have a hundred temptations to withstand, but whenever you are tempted may you say, 'How shall I do this great wickedness, and sin against *my* God?' May God call upon you early by His grace, my dear W."

To E. and M.† she said, "God bless you, my dear girls; you have been kind and good girls to me; always read your Bible, never neglect it, and pray that God may bless it to you, and then you will be happy. Be amiable, and you will be sure to gain friends. Seek first the kingdom of God and His righteousness, and all else shall be added unto you, for godliness is profitable unto all things, having promise of the life that now is, and of that which is to come." At the same time she pressed the duty of reading the Scriptures daily on H., and reminded her of the Gospel privileges which she had enjoyed here.

* Her only surviving son, since dead.

† Her daughters, since dead.

April 11.—My dearest aunt has been decidedly worse to-day. Yesterday, feeling extremely weak, the flesh seemed to shrink from the swellings of Jordan; but to-day she has been mercifully relieved from any recurrence of the feeling. I mentioned to her the passage, "The name of the Lord is a strong tower; the righteous runneth into it, and is safe." "Yes," she said, "and, when I can go nowhere else, I can find refuge there."

Monday night, May 8.—Since I last wrote, dear aunt has been gradually growing worse. On Friday, reviving a little, she said to me, "Is it possible that I am so near heaven? One moment in heaven will make amends for all. I know my Saviour, I love Him; and I cannot bear the thought of another disappointment." At another time, in reply, when I asked her how she was, "Going home. I have been comforted ever since you read that piece to me (referring to the account of the peaceful death of Bishop Cowper, in the *Church of England Magazine*); and, when I go to sleep, if not too sleepy, I commend myself to my heavenly Father. Oh, my heavenly Father, how I love Him! How my love to Him is increased! Perfectly happy, perfectly! oh, my Saviour, whether Thou take me now or not. Perfectly! Oh, how happy! Come, Lord Jesus, come quickly! My Saviour and my God! That is the sweetest sound that ever strikes my ear. I am ready, quite ready for His summons; longing to be gone; but hope that I am willing to wait His time."

On Friday, the 12th, she was evidently much worse; her medical attendant entering, said, "You will soon meet your little boy." "Yes," she replied, "I shall soon meet my Saviour, who died for me;" and then expressed her hope that she might meet Mr. F. there.

Throughout the day she appeared dying, and was frequently saying, "Heaven, heaven!" In the evening she said to E., "No delusion, my dear E., no delusion." She spoke with the greatest composure of her approaching death, and desired us to pray earnestly that she might soon be released. During the latter part of the evening, I sat by her bedside, conversing with her; she was longing to be gone, and full of light. About twelve o'clock her breathing became more oppressed. She said to me, "My dear J., I wish you had seen several persons die; you would then know whether I am dying. I think I am dying." Her breathing became still more difficult; we called up all the family but the two little ones, and all stood round the bed, watching for her departure. I held her hand in mine, and for a long time, when I pressed it, she returned the pressure, till at length she ceased to exhibit consciousness. For some time after this I supported her in my arms, and then again laid her on the pillows; she gave one groan as we changed her position; in a few minutes after, her breathing gradually became fainter, and at half-past three in the morning of May 13th, 1837, she entered into her so-long-wished-for rest, without a sigh or a struggle.

In reference to this, and all such death-bed scenes, may we not adopt the language of the poet:—

"Go, child of darkness, see a Christian die:
No horror pales his lip, or rolls his eye;
No dreadful doubts or dreamy terrors start
The hope religion pillows on his heart,
When with a dying hand he waves adieu
To all who love so well and weep so true.

Meek, as an infant to the mother's breast
Turns fondly longing for its wonted rest,
He pants for where congenial spirits stray,
Turns to his God, and sighs his soul away."

CHAPTER XXI.

HEAVENLY ZEAL—THE CHRISTIAN'S ANXIETY TO IMPART—ALFRED'S FIRST ATTEMPT AT AUTHORSHIP—HIS SUCCESS AND SUBSEQUENT DEFEAT—THE REVIEW AND ITS EFFECTS—ALFRED GOES TO LONDON—LETTER OF RECOMMENDATION—TIMIDITY—OBTAINS A SITUATION—COMMENCES BUSINESS—UNDERTAKES AN EDITORSHIP—BEREAVEMENTS.

ZEAL is an early fruit of grace in the heart. The very reverse of human nature—which wants to *obtain* and to *hold*—divine grace is no sooner given than its possessor wants to *impart.* He longs for others to partake of his peace, his pleasure, his prospects. Feelings of this kind actuated young Alfred, when God was pleased to "turn him from darkness to light, and from the power of sin and Satan unto God." Years before, he had thought how he should like to write a book; and now, with a fresh spring and a holy impulse, he thought to make the attempt. He wrote a little 32mo, addressed to youth, "Upon the great importance of, and benefits arising from, seeking the Lord whilst young." Having finished the MS., he sent it to John, who had it printed. It took well, and some four or five thousand copies were sold in a few weeks. Pleased with his success—and no doubt a vast deal more proud of it than he at the time was aware—Alfred soon made a second attempt at authorship; but a fellow Sunday-school-teacher procuring an early copy of his new production, urged a London reviewer to "cut it up." For such a criticism our author—being scarcely seventeen at the time—was not prepared. He had no notion of being so severely handled, and very soon made his exit from off the publishing stage. Many a year passed before he ventured as an author to appear in public again. His next effort, however, was altogether as favourably received. It was a story founded on fact, and soon ran through an edition. But a little prior to this, Alfred, at the close of his term, left the country for London. With a letter of recommendation, he presented himself to the principal of a large establishment. "I cannot comply with this," said he, "unless I supplant some one else." Alfred would not hear of this; and, his heart failing him when glancing round at the extent of the building, he felt pleased rather than otherwise at the result of his application. He was very little in the TRY-mood at the time. A fortnight after, he called again, merely to say that he had done so, when the principal offered him a situation. Again his heart misgave him; and but for the kindness of the gentleman in question, would most certainly have declined the offer. That gentleman perhaps remembered his own entrance in life—first, as a shop-boy, from which he rose to the head of the establishment, leaving it for his present more extensive one, with a capital of many thousand pounds. It is well when employers are mindful of their former position, and act accordingly. Encouraged by the gentleness of the party in question, Alfred entered that establishment; he *tried*, and in three weeks occupied one of the most desirable positions in it. If he had had his choice among the hundred and fifty engaged there, the place to which he was appointed would have been the one he would have selected. He remained in that situation some three or four years, gaining much practical knowledge; and afterwards commenced business on his own account, beginning by degrees, and enlarging according to circumstances, until he occupied for some ten years the premises spoken of in a previous chapter.

There was a circumstance occurred in the early part of Alfred's business career, which, perhaps, ought not to be omitted, as it may serve to inculcate both a useful and encouraging lesson. Alfred was now but a young tradesman, commencing only upon a comparatively small scale, — a neatly-arranged bookseller's shop, with a pretty selection of books and stationery. The printing-office contained only one press, to begin with, and a small but well-chosen set of types. He was, however, as most young tradesmen are, anxious about the issue of his enterprise. At first, he had but little to do in the printing-office, and but very few customers in the shop. Habitually prone to look on the dark side of things, he began to ask how was his beloved young wife and himself to live, and, in case of a family, how were they to be maintained? He was at this time living in the outskirts of London—some three to four miles from the City. One evening he had walked into town, to discharge a bill for some books, and, thinking it was a good opportunity, ventured to solicit of the publisher some printing. He was advanced in years; and, though naturally a man of the kindest heart, was at times subject to excitement. The request (though modestly put) irritated him; and his reply was such as to send Alfred homeward with a depressed and most sorrowful heart. Satan (that arch enemy of God and man) took advantage of his depression, and suggested that ruin would be the result, and that speedily. His pain of mind that evening was extreme. Upon reaching home, his even-minded and most devoted wife said, in reference to a poor man who had just left the shop, "I think B—— is very low to-night. I wish you would step after him and give him a shilling." The man referred to was very poor, with a large family of nine children. He was a gardener by trade, but often without employment, and his wife earned what she could as a laundress. Such a request at such a moment seemed rather unseemly to Alfred; but his wife was always more prudent and far-seeing than he. Thought he, "Well, though this is only making bad worse, God forbid that I should check your kind feelings;" so off he ran after the man, and slipped the shilling into his hand. "Who sent this?" said he. "A friend," was the reply. The very next morning's post brought a letter from one of the firm of the publishing house just now referred to, requesting Alfred to call

about some printing. He did so, and found it was an estimate required for the printing of a good-sized volume. His estimate was accepted; and, from that day till the time he relinquished business—some eleven years afterwards—he was never an hour without work from that house. He received thousands upon thousands from that firm, and that simple circumstance laid the foundation of all his future course.

Hence, dear youthful reader, is it not clear that there is One above who not only watches over, but is fully acquainted with all the secret workings of our minds? Whilst on the one hand His word says, "Your heavenly Father knoweth ye have need of all these things before ye ask Him," and that "not a sparrow falleth to the ground without your Father's knowledge;" so likewise does it declare that he that "giveth to the poor lendeth to the Lord;" that "there is that scattereth, and yet increaseth, and there is that withholdeth more than is meet, and it tendeth to poverty." Again we see that all hearts are in God's hands, and that He can, and oftentimes does, overrule the most discouraging of circumstances for the well-being of those who seek Him. It was the very sharpness and irritability of the old gentleman in question that led him to reflect, and made him anxious immediately afterwards to show a different spirit. During the years that he and Alfred subsequently transacted business together, the latter never remembered hearing an unkind word fall from his lips.

After a season, much domestic sorrow fell to Alfred's portion. At the suggestion of a beloved friend, he—in addition to the superintendence of an extensive printing and publishing establishment—undertook an editorship that involved him in the necessity of a special course of training. As it has been repeatedly said, Alfred's impulsive temperament needed discipline. Apart from this, the position to which he was now called, made such discipline the more indispensable. That discipline he had —in trial upon trial—temptation after temptation—one bereavement rapidly following another. First, a sweet boy; then two lovely girls: next the object of his youthful love, and devoted companion of his riper years, was smitten. Consumption wasted her delicate frame; after a few months' illness, she died. So frequently and

within so short a period was the family grave opened, that the clergyman of the parish (familiar as he was with such scenes) was greatly affected by it; and, though in other respects a stranger, was moved with deepest sympathy. One incident with regard to the last interment may not be unworthy of note, in proof of God's timely remembrance of the bereaved and afflicted. All of Alfred's loved ones had now been cut off except *one*—that a dear, dear boy of from four to five years of age. Upon the brink of the family and oft-opened grave, stood Alfred and this last fond relic of his once happy household. "Not going to bury *me*," said he, in his childish unconsciousness of what a funeral was: as with his bereaved parent he stepped out of the mourning coach. "Not going to bury *me*," said he again, as they stooped o'er the grave, to take a last look, and bid a lingering farewell. Oh, what an appeal was *that!* How timely! One remained—and though but one—it served to remind Alfred that he had duties to perform which neither cowardice nor selfishness should make him willing to forego.

CHAPTER XXII.

JOHN'S WISH TO ENTER THE MINISTRY—ITS IMPORTANCE—A MATTER BETWEEN GOD AND THE SOUL—EARNESTNESS INDISPENSABLE—HIS FORMER ANXIETY ABOUT HIS SOUL—A WEEPING NIGHT—HIS ALARM WHILST BATHING—PEACE BY THE BLOOD OF JESUS—HIS ORDINATION AND FIRST SERMON.

VERY soon after taking his fellowship, it would seem that John's mind disposed him to the ministry of the Church of England. Doubtless it had long turned in that direction; but it was a matter so sacred as seldom to be touched upon; and one which had specially to do with God and his own conscience. He felt—as indeed every Divinity-student or Minister ought to feel—that of all positions, that of the Ministry is the most solemn.

At an earlier date, he had expressed to Alfred his great anxiety about the welfare of his soul. He had one evening attended with his grandpapa a week-evening service. Upon retiring to rest, he was greatly distressed, and wept much. Upon Alfred's asking the cause of his grief, he said, "His grandpa had been much affected by a verse in one of the hymns:

> "Soon shall I pass the gloomy vale,
> Soon all my mortal powers must fail;
> Oh may my last expiring breath,
> His loving-kindness sing in death."

And "he thought if his dear grandpa felt such concern and anxiety in the prospect of death, what ought *he* to feel?"

Again, in the night but one after the death of Alfred's beloved sister before referred to, John roused him from his slumbers, being at the time in such distress of mind and bitterness of soul, that he could not sleep. "Oh, suppose it had been *me*," said he; "supposing *I* had died, instead of dear Mary."

Once, too, when bathing, Alfred was standing on the rocks, and John said he would spring in a little out of his depth. He did so, and, his courage instantly failing him, he screamed to his companion, with a look of intense terror, fearfully alarmed at the thought of death.

But, at the time of which we now speak, he had been raised to hope and confidence. He had in very deed "fled for refuge to lay hold upon the hope set before him in the Gospel." He knew and believed "that the blood of Jesus Christ (God's dear Son) cleanseth from all sin." And, having felt its virtue, he longed to declare to others its peace-producing power. It was under these feelings, when visiting Alfred in London, he said to him one day, "Perhaps the next time I see you I shall be a Minister."

After a season this wish was realized. Having duly undergone the Bishop's examination, upon a Sunday

morning, prior to the usual public service, he was ordained. Alfred was present to witness from the gallery that deeply solemn ceremony. Much he felt there when he contemplated in that dear young man—his nephew—the child of so many prayers—the loved companion of his early days—what God had wrought! And when, afterwards, he mingled with the congregation, and, looking up, beheld in the preacher one whose father's dying breathings were that his orphan boy might grow up to be, not only a *good* man, but a *useful* one, Alfred could but acknowledge and admire the goodness and mercy of a prayer-hearing and a prayer-answering God.

Oh that many of the dear young people who read this little work may be encouraged by its simple and truthful record to look to the Lord—to plead with the Lord—to cry, "My Father, be thou the Guide of my youth." Oh what a blessing will attend such! Blessings now—blessings for ever! God a Guide—a Father—a Friend here, and an everlasting Portion hereafter! Unbounded satisfaction will all such as seek and serve Him enjoy. They shall know how true it is that "Godliness hath the promise of the life that now is, as well as of that which is to come."

None out of the myriads who have known and served the Lord ever regretted their choice, whilst millions upon millions have deplored, when too late, their neglect of and indifference and enmity to those things which alone could administer to their present well-being and their everlasting consolation.

CHAPTER XXIII.

JOHN AS CURATE OF BARNWELL—HIS INTEREST IN THE PEOPLE—THE CHARACTER OF HIS PREACHING.

JOHN laboured for some time among the poor as curate of the densely-populated parish of Barnwell, near Cambridge. By them he was much and deservedly beloved. None could have had their interest more at heart. God had dealt very tenderly with John. He had not been called to go down into such dismal depths aa many; consequently he knew less of the foulness of the human heart. But there was much affectionate concern about his ministry, notwithstanding. With him it was not a cold lip-service, but a heartfelt anxiety on behalf of his people. Though a scholar himself, there was no attempt at display; no vain show of words; but plain, pointed, practical expositions, interwoven with simple and telling illustrations, and solemn and affectionate appeals to the hearts and consciences of his hearers.

For example, in a small volume of sermons published since his death, in his opening remarks upon 1 Tim. i. 15, he says:

Suppose a messenger should go into Norwich* Hospital with tidings of an infallible physician; or into the county gaol with news of the coming of the prince for a gaol-delivery, with what feelings of joy, think you, the sick, or the prisoners, would hear the tidings? Better tidings, a Physician really infallible—more joyful news, a Prince truly come! Why is there not joy? Suppose the sick person in the hospital senseless; or suppose that the prisoners in the gaol had found so many methods to while away the time, that they had become fond of their bondage, careless of their doom—What then?

Again, upon "Repentance," he says:

But what I want you clearly to understand is that repentance, in its large extent, is something very different from this, something far deeper; there may be all this without one grain of true repentance, there may be real repentance without any such formal act. Repentance is the source from which the act springs. To see the pains which many take before the Lord's Supper, and the way in which the heart, like the bow unstrung, springs back to its former amusements and worldly pleasures afterwards, reminds me strongly of Fuller's quaint, but forcible, illustration of the children in their

* The next town to his parish.

new shoes—"You will see them in a day or two walking in the thickest of the mire, whereas at first they were fearful of soiling even the sole."

Moreover, in his illustrations upon Luke xiii. 24, he remarks:

1. Suppose a door strait and low, and a man rides up to it on horseback. Can he enter?—Nay, he must dismount. Can he go in with head erect and haughty brow?—Nay, he must STOOP. Now the *self-righteous man* will not do this. He cannot consent to enter heaven upon the humiliating terms which the Gospel requires. What! must he place no trust in his moral rectitude, his fair and upright dealings, his charitable distributions, his amiable deportment, his religious duties? Must he be willing to cast all these away as to any *claim* which they can give him on the divine favour? Must he renounce *self* as well as *sin?* Must he come to Christ on the same footing as the openly guilty and profane? He cannot do it—he cannot stoop. Naaman-like, he turns away in a rage, and thinks his Abanas and Pharpars better than all the waters of Israel. Dear brethren, this will not do. This was the ruin of the Pharisees of old (Rom. x. 3), "They being ignorant, &c., have not *submitted*," &c. It is a *low* door, my brethren, as well as a *strait* one.

2. But see again, there is a man with a great bundle. He has reached the door, can he get in?—Nay, his bundle is too great; he must leave the bundle outside the door, if he would enter within the *strait* gate. In plain words, my brethren, you cannot carry your sins with you, if you would set out on a course of vital godliness: the door is too narrow for sins and sinner too. No sinner need be excluded if he come casting away

his sins; but one sin *cherished* will keep him out. What, then, is to become of covetousness, love of pleasure, worldliness? They must be cast away. How many have "*sought* to enter in," but "have not been able" from this cause,—sin loved, sin cherished, iniquity regarded in the heart, have kept them out. Herod-like, they have done many things, *but kept Herodias.*

3. But look again. Suppose you saw a man labouring with infinite pains to break a way through a stone wall, when there was a gate close by. You would, perhaps, smile at his folly, or you would, perhaps, try to dissuade him from the useless task. But it may be he has never seen the door, and has had no one to direct him to it, and he labours on, worn and weary, in the hope of forcing his way through at last, and all without success. There are some who are doing this in the vain endeavour to make a way to heaven for themselves; perhaps they despise the right door, perhaps they have never heard of it. They *seek*—nay, they *strive*—but they get no advantage by the one or the other. This is the case with those who impose austerities upon themselves—the hair-shirt, and the scourge, and the pointed cross; the neglecting of the body, and the like methods of self-mortification followed out by the devotees of the Church of Rome, or the self-torturers of India. What shall we say to them? Alas! theirs is labour in vain. Some may do all this to gratify pride, to gain a name for holiness; such are most hateful to God. Some, in the darkness of ignorance, may have never heard of the true way, and would listen with joy to the cheering tidings, could they but hear them. Oh, how are such to be pitied! and how will such rise up in judgment against us, if knowing the way, as revealed to us in the

Gospel, and preached to us from Sabbath to Sabbath, we be found neglecting to enter in! "Many shall seek to enter in, but shall not be able." Are we among the many? How is it with us—are we among the strivers, or the seekers? Shall we be found in heaven at last?

CHAPTER XXIV.

ALFRED'S DESIRE FOR THE MINISTRY—SOLACE UNDER BEREAVEMENT — APPARENTLY INSURMOUNTABLE DIFFICULTIES—HIS FORMER SCRUPLES REMOVED—PROPOSAL TO GO TO IRELAND—HIS REPUGNANCE—HIS WILLINGNESS—HIS INTEREST THENCEFORWARD IN THE SISTER-ISLE—GOD'S WORK DONE BY HIMSELF.

ENGAGED as Alfred was to some extent in the Lord's work, in the conducting of a religious journal of very long standing, yet he panted to be more exclusively occupied in the Lord's vineyard, and the very idea reconciled him in great measure to the distressing bereavements to which he had been called to submit. But there appeared insuperable difficulties in the way; and the object was so truly sacred, that in this matter his old motto TRY was out of the question. At first—and for many years—he shrank from the weight and responsibility; but, when the Lord rebuked his fears—assured him of *His* all-sufficiency—and "made him willing in the day of His power," there seemed not the slightest human probability of its being brought about. How was *he* to be released from the claims of a large and anxious establishment, and enter the Ministry of the Church of England?

A beloved brother in the Lord had proposed Ireland

to him; to this he gave mentally a direct negative. But, shortly after, he was walking through one of the squares of London, when the Lord was pleased to commune with his anxious mind. He was led back in review of "all the way by which the Lord had led him," and forward in hope and assurance of what He was able still to accomplish.

He saw, as in a moment, all the path by which he had been led from the time he left his father's house up to that present hour. What "goodness and mercy had followed him." How kind the Lord had been; how watchful! He had been provided for, notwithstanding all his numberless misgivings; he had been preserved in dangers great and manifold; he had been rescued and succoured in seasons of temptation and trial. Hence, as he mused, he could but exclaim,

"When all Thy mercies, O my God,
My rising soul surveys;
Transported with the view, I'm lost
In wonder, love, and praise.

"When in the slippery paths of youth
With heedless steps I ran,
Thine arm, unseen, conveyed me safe,
And led me up to man.

"Ten thousand thousand precious gifts,
My daily thanks employ;
Nor is the least a cheerful heart,
That tastes those gifts with joy.

"Through every period of my life,
Thy goodness I'll adore;
And after death, in distant worlds,
Thy mercy still explore.

"Through all eternity to Thee,
A joyful song I'll raise;
But, oh! eternity's too short
To utter all Thy praise."

Then, as he looked forward, it was as though the Lord said to him, "If I have been with you in the *past*, can

I not be equally with you for the *future?* If I *have* provided and protected, can I not do so still? Can *Ireland* be more strange to you than *London* was, when I brought you up, a country youth and inexperienced?" From that moment all scruples about Ireland were removed, and a greater interest felt in it than about any other part of the world. From that moment the welfare of the Sister-Isle was laid deeply upon his heart. He longed to be sent there upon his Lord and Master's business. Still there was not the slightest prospect of its coming to pass, nor durst Alfred move in the matter. However it may behove us as creatures to TRY in earthly things, yet *God's* work will be done by God Himself. Of this it may be distinctly said, "Not by might, nor by power, but by my Spirit, saith the Lord of hosts." God will neither be hurried nor interrupted in *His* work. And it is for us, as creatures, to "Stand still, and see the salvation of the Lord."

Again and again did Alfred *try* to forget his inclination for the ministry, and to immerse himself more intensely in the business of the world, but disappointment—losses and crosses—were sure to follow.

At length, indirectly through the medium of the work before referred to, and by a most remarkable train of providences, in which the Lord's hand was most plain, Alfred received an invitation to Ireland.

CHAPTER XXV.

JOHN'S DELICACY—SPENDS THREE WINTERS ABROAD—VISIT TO HIS EARLY FRIEND AND COMPANION—THE VACANT PARISH—SINGULAR COINCIDENCE—JOHN'S APPOINTMENT.

ON account of his health—which was somewhat failing—John was obliged, for three successive winters, to seek a warmer climate. Twice he went to Madeira, and once to the south of France. He had now returned, and was upon a visit to his early friend and companion in the neighbourhood of London.

During this visit the TRY-principle was singularly put to the test. A most valuable living had some months previously become vacant. None but a Fellow of his College could be appointed. In prospect of its falling in, the lady of the patron had made certain inquiries about the several Fellows. Without his knowledge, John had been brought before her; but, on account of a political bias on the part of her husband, she would not venture to suggest his nomination. One evening, a note was brought by a mounted messenger from the said Countess, addressed to Alfred, enclosing one for John. It was to this effect: "The Earl has just written to me to say, 'The living of ——— is lost, in consequence of the delay of a letter, which has been traversing the country. The parish lapses the day after to-morrow, and therefore there is no time to appoint.' I have (continued the Countess) written by a special messenger to say *I* do not consider the case hopeless, for I happen to know of a most desirable clergyman to present to the living;" at the same time giving the name of John D. Lane.

"I will see your Ladyship in the morning," wrote John, in reply. "Go at once," said Alfred. He went, and at a late hour in the evening, returned, exclaiming, ere he had time to alight from the carriage, "I have the living." The Countess's messenger met the Earl as he was descending the steps of his town-house. He took the letter—read it—returned to his drawing-room, and there and then wrote the appointment of J. D. L. to a living in the diocese of Norwich, worth at that time upwards of £1,200 a-year.

CHAPTER XXVI.

JOURNEY TO IRELAND—ITS UNBOUNDED SATISFACTION—THE LORD'S PRECIOUSNESS OF THE WORD—ITS TIMELY AND PERSONAL APPLICATION.

ALFRED, on the 4th of November, 1846, left his loved family circle, and set out for the Emerald Isle. All was new and strange. It was like commencing life afresh. Most peculiar were his feelings as he stepped on board the steamer at Liverpool, to cross for the first time the Irish Sea. And yet that railway journey and voyage exceeded in real heart-felt pleasure and satisfaction everything he had ever known.

He felt as though he was sent upon *the Lord's* errand, and as though the Lord would, in consequence, sustain and bless. His presence was felt, and His word was most precious. They were most distressing scenes into the very midst of which he was going, for the never-to-be-forgotten famine of 1846-7 was then raging in all its destructiveness; but God proved Himself to be all-sufficient.

He had said to the trembling and reluctant one before-

hand, "Have not I commanded thee?" "I have set before thee an open door, and no man can shut it;" "Certainly I will be with thee." These assurances of divine counsel and direction sufficed. In the strength of the Lord God of Israel, that feeble one went forth, encouraged, moreover, by the word spoken unto Gideon,

"Go in this thy might;" and followed up very speedily, when treading upon the Irish shores, with, "There is no man that hath left house, or parents, or brethren, or wife, or children, for the kingdom of God's sake, who shall not receive manifold more in this present time, and in the world to come life everlasting."

Oh, how precious are the Scriptures when the Holy Ghost condescends to apply them to our hearts, and adapt them to the trials or anxieties we may at the time be passing through. May the Lord make the youthful reader thus (Samuel-like) to "hear" the Lord speaking through and by His word. This will lessen care; this dispel dread and darkness and doubt; this possess the soul with at least a measure of that holy confidence which the Psalmist enjoyed when he said, "Though I walk through the valley of the shadow of death, I will fear no evil, for *Thou art with me:* Thy rod and Thy staff they comfort me."

And should the Lord's work be laid upon the heart of my dear young readers, though it may be a self-denying work, and perhaps involve a separation from kindred and friends, and the sacrifice of earthly prospects or mere human advantages, yet such have no need to fear or despond. God will make up the loss, and do for them "exceeding abundantly above all that they can ask or think."

As intimated in a previous page, if none ever regretted the choice of the *precepts* of the Lord, so none ever were sorry for having walked in the *pathway* of the Lord.

Where His precepts prescribe, His providence protects. To such as walk in the ways of the Lord, there is the realization of a peace, a pleasure, a prospect, that as far outvies all that this poor perishing world can afford, as light exceeds darkness, or heaven surpasses hell. The contrast is inconceivable; the satisfaction indescribable; the enjoyment only to be exceeded by a happiness that has no admixture of sin, in heaven's eternal and uninterrupted glory.

Oh, then, that my dear young reader may have grace to "choose that good part which cannot be taken away from him;" and, having done so, may it be his daily mercy to cry, "Lord, what wilt Thou have me to do?"

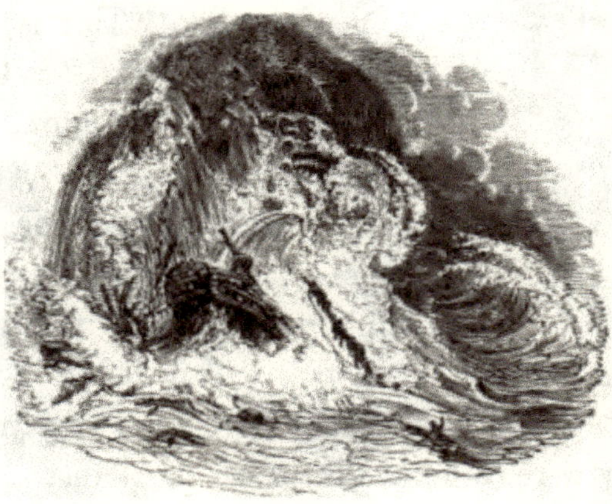

CHAPTER XXVII.

THE PRESENT A WORLD OF CHANGES—"NO ABIDING CITY HERE"—JOHN'S SEVERE ILLNESS—HIS LETTERS—HIS DEATH.

REST is reserved for the world that is to come, and not for the world that now is. "This is not your rest, it is polluted," is the plain language of Scripture. "Here we have no continuing city." "Set your affections," therefore, said the Apostle, "on things above, and not on things on the earth." "Vanity of vanities, saith the preacher; all is vanity." This lesson both John and Alfred had been taught from their very youth up; but they were to have still further proof that

> "We've no abiding city here;
> This may distress the worldling's mind,
> But should not cost the saint a tear,
> Who hopes a better rest to find.

"We've no abiding city here;
 Sad truth were this to be our home;
But let this thought our spirits cheer,
 We seek a city yet to come.

"We've no abiding city here;
 We seek a city out of sight:
Zion its name—the Lord is there;
 It shines with everlasting light."

John had scarcely been appointed three years to his new and important parish, ere fresh proofs of his extreme delicacy began to show themselves.

Within a few days of his arrival in Ireland, his early friend and companion received the following letter :—

Nov. 20*th*, 1846.

MY DEAREST A.,

The Lord be praised that you have been carried in safety to your present post of duty: He will direct and support you still. I have been comforted lately by these cheering words, "The steps of a good man are ordered by the Lord, and in His way is his delight." You and I know in what sense only we can lay claim to the *character*—but being, as we are sometimes privileged to hope, *believers in Jesus*, how graciously does this intimation of the Lord's tender interest in our concerns serve to cheer and support us. Not merely the general route, nor the end at which we are to arrive, but the particular *steps* of the way, all are ordered by infinite wisdom and unbounded love; and, as you loved to watch your little David, when he first began to walk, and took delight in his progress as he began to venture with tottering steps, so does the Lord delight in watching and ordering our way. How quickly your hand was stretched out when a little inequality in the carpet made you fear your boy would trip! so it is with the Lord. Oh, for more faith to trust Him; to stay upon His faithfulness and love! If He gives us the privilege of delighting in *His* way, how sweet an assurance is this that He delights in *ours!*

But I am running on, and shall soon have but little room left for telling you how much I was interested in the few details you sent me. Your account of your little flock in the mountains was very full of interest. I do not wonder at your weeping with them. Yours was a precious subject, too, with which to commence your ministry among them—"*good* tidings of *great* joy unto *all* people." Look at the three adjectives: what a fulness there is in the whole!

Now, you will want to hear about me. I have, indeed, been very unwell, though, through the mercy of God, with no alarming, or indeed very serious symptoms. I have been under Mr. B.'s hands a fortnight to-morrow. His remedies have, through the mercy of God, been greatly blessed; and, what with two blisters on the chest, and continual medicines, my cough is now greatly lessened, and I trust I am altogether better. However, I have been confined to the house, and indeed to my bedroom and study, and there is little doubt, I think, that this attack will lead to my early remove to Torquay, if not to a warmer climate. It has been in prospect of this that the verse I alluded to at the opening of my letter proved so comforting.

The Lord direct and uphold you. May He keep you from all evil, and make you the means of extensive good! Remember me in your approaches to the throne of grace;—how much I need the prayers of God's dear children! Faith, love, and every grace, are sadly low in me.

Yours ever affectionately,

J. D. Lane.

To an uncle he wrote, a few days after, as follows:—

Nov. 25th, 1846.

My dear E.,

I am writing on your birthday, the day on which you are forty-two years old. Your birthday and mine fall so close together, that the remembrance of one is pretty sure to bring that of the other. If spared until Friday, I shall be thirty-four. Curious enough, Mr. B.'s birthday is the same, he is thirty-two; and another, W. D., the clergyman of R. The Lord grant us all a birthday blessing! He knows your wants and ours—knows what is really best for us all. We, in our short-sightedness, should probably ask for health, and freedom from trials and bereavements, and the light of His countenance. He, in His wisdom, may perhaps give us sickness, affliction, desertion, and conflict. Oh, He knows best! He knows how to bring down and how to raise up—how to cause us to grow up into Christ—how to make us "grow in grace and in the knowledge of our Lord and Saviour Jesus Christ."

What a mercy it is that we have "a faithful Creator," wise and compassionate, One who knoweth our frame, who remembereth that we are dust. What then is our wisdom? Why to roll ourselves upon Him—to refer everything back to Him again—to ask Him to deal with us according to His loving mercy, and to let our will be His. Those are beautiful words, I know not whence they came—

'Oh may my will be swallowed up in Thine,
That I may do Thy will in doing mine."

My illness has been, I think, an attack of influenza, taking an obstinate form from my tendency to disease of the chest. I am still a prisoner to my bedroom and study, although, as we all hope, decidedly better. My cough is, however, obstinate, the season being so much against me. It will probably lead to my early removal southwards, but whether to Torquay or to Ventnor (which I should prefer), or farther south still, I am waiting for the gracious providence of God to determine.

Yours ever affectionately,

J. D. L.

Again to Alfred he writes :—

November 30, 1846.

MY DEAR A.,

I am looking out with much interest for a second letter from you. The Lord grant that you may be still sustained and comforted in your work, and may see plainly that He is going before you, compassing you round about and following you. You must tell me what your daily duties are, and how you have been able to go forward with your lectures on the mountains.

You will be wishing to hear about my health. My cough and expectoration still remain very considerable; and although, through the mercy of God, my pulse is quiet and appetite good, and I am free from fever, they are still so obstinate that I much fear nothing but a warmer climate will remove them. I had hoped Torquay would have proved sufficient, but do not know what to say. I am to have another blister this evening. However, dear A., I am in the Lord's hands; may He do with me as shall be really for my good. I want more of *realizing* faith. I am not anxious, neither am I enjoying a sense of the Lord's favour. Remember me in your prayers.

Your ever affectionate,

J. D. L.

Under date Feb. 13, 1847, he writes again to the same:—

MY DEAR A.,

Time passes, and I am writing this within a day of the middle of the month of February. I have been the Lord's prisoner to the house about fourteen weeks (save one little walk of ten minutes on a fine morning in December), and to my room between eight and nine. On the whole it is surprising that, with such a cough as I have had during the whole of the longer period, and with so great an amount of expectoration, leaving out of the case the serious discharges of blood, it is quite surprising that my constitution has held out as it has. In fact, I have scarcely a symptom which may be called constitutional, notwithstanding the certainty of considerable disease in the structure of the lungs. There seems now, I think, to be a prospect of the Lord's sparing me again for a time; but He knows what He is about to do with me, and I hope I can say with sincerity—

> "My times are in Thy hand;
> My God! I wish them there."

Every week passed without my becoming worse is so much gained, as it brings me nearer to the fine weather of May and June. Three weeks ago I was suffering greatly from severe paroxysms of coughing; so severe, indeed, as to appear to render it certain that hæmorrhage must follow. I was obliged in consequence to have four leeches on my chest twice, and to proceed on a lowering system—low diet and reducing medicines; notwithstanding these measures the expectoration was more than once discoloured. I trust, however, the means used have been blessed, and that the crisis has passed for the present. My cough is comparatively quiet, and I have felt better these few days than for some time past.

Now I have told you much about myself. I do rejoice that you are so earnestly and usefully engaged in the best of work, and have many times felt comforted with the thought, that, if the Lord was going to remove me, He was going to raise up you, and perhaps my dear W——,* as labourers in His vineyard. O that you may be far more devoted, far more in earnest, far more spiritual, and far more useful than ever I have been! I want much to hear of your progress. The Lord bless you.

Ever affectionately yours,

J. D. L.

To his uncle E., he again wrote:—

February 25th, 1847.

My dear E.,

* * * * *

There are some things which I trust are more deeply impressed on my mind by this affliction—the Lord grant they may be more and more! One is, how absolutely and entirely faith is the Lord's gift. It is so utterly im-

* W. afterwards became a minister of the Church of England, and has since died.

possible to exercise it without His gracious putting forth of power. My own utter helplessness, too, is another thing which I hope He is teaching me; not even a good thought can I set in exercise, or bring to effect, without Him. I know all this, and have felt it, but seem to have felt more in this illness.

What I want to realize more is Christ—His love, His person, His offices—the reality of His union with me, and mine with Him. I can tell something about these things, and seem to understand something of them; but I want to realize them more in my daily experience. Do you not remember how dear grandma used to say, "To whom coming?" She used to love to dwell on that text. Now this is that I want to realize more—daily, hourly coming to Jesus—drawing from His fulness, resting in His love, strengthened by His power, living by His life. I thank God that in the latter days of my ministry I was led to feel more and more the importance of keeping Christ prominent in my sermons. Oh, if the Lord should ever grant me the privilege again, may Christ be more and more "all in all" in my own heart, my own walk, and in all my ministrations!

Ever yours,

J. D. L.

But his wishes again to appear in public—a messenger for his Master—were never realized. He grew weaker and weaker; and at times suffered considerably from darkness of mind and gloomy apprehension as to his state. At other times the Lord would appear; and then he would say, "It is *my* infirmity. *The Lord* changeth not: He is the same yesterday, and to-day, and for ever."

There was one circumstance, however, within a few days of the close of his career, which cheered him greatly. He had been very dark in his mind for some days, when the Lord was pleased to send him a testimony that melted his heart into sweetest gratitude, and afforded him renewed evidence of His gracious favour. A young man, in his very circumstances—*dying of consumption*—wrote to the Religious Tract Society, to beg that they would inform the unknown writer of a certain tract (of which, it seems, dear John was the author), that he had found a copy of it under a hedge; that the reading of it had been blessed to his conversion; and that he was now dying in the embrace of the truths it contained.

This was a timely—and a very precious—mercy.

A few days before his departure, he said to a beloved relative, "If I should be deprived of my reason before I am taken, remember it will make no difference. I am upon the Rock." This, it would appear, was a prior intimation from the Lord; for, during the three days immediately preceding his death, he had not, apparently, a lucid moment.

He fell asleep on the 27th of April, 1847, in the thirty-fifth year of his age.

Soon after his decease, a subscription was set on foot in the parish wherein he had laboured as curate for some four or five years previously; and with the proceeds, a tablet, containing a suitable inscription, was placed on the walls of Christ Church, Barnwell.

CHAPTER XXVIII.

THE WISDOM AND GOODNESS OF GOD—ALFRED'S FIRST SUNDAY IN IRELAND—COTTAGE LECTURE—THE FAMINE AND ITS SAD SCENES—A VISIT TO CAMBRIDGE—BARNWELL CHURCH—THE OBJECT OF THIS WORK—CONCLUSION.

HOW wise, as well as tender and gracious, are the Lord's dealings! Had Alfred's loved friend and bosom-companion been re-removed at another time, or under other circumstances, his loss would have been almost insupportable. But as it was, the mind of Alfred was at least in great measure diverted by other and most important matters. On the Sunday after his arrival in Ireland, he was privileged to commence his cottage lectures upon the mountains. Most affecting were those scenes, and deeply interesting those little assemblies. His opening subject was (Luke ii. 10, 11),

"Behold, I bring you good tidings of great joy, which shall be to all people; for unto you is born this day, in the city of David, a Saviour, which is Christ the Lord."

Within a few days of his arrival, he was brought into closest contact with the dreaded famine-scenes; and, in the good providence of God, was enabled, through the kindness and liberality of friends in England, to administer largely and for many months to the pressing necessities of the people.

The reader may conceive of what were Alfred's feelings on one occasion, a year or two after his ordination. He went to Cambridge, for the purpose of spending a few hours with the beloved friend and relative referred to in page 91, who was then passing through College, preparatory to the Ministry. It happened to be service-night at Barnwell Church; and an invitation was sent to Alfred to preach. His former visit to Cambridge was directly brought to his mind. That death-bed scene described in page 96, when John's aunt, and Alfred's beloved but dying sister, turned to the latter, and said, with an emphasis that can never be forgotten, "This light affliction, which is but for a moment, worketh for us a far more exceeding and eternal weight of glory." "What more suitable for a text?" thought Alfred. With these words he entered the pulpit so recently occupied by his devoted friend and early companion. Before him were those who had so often listened to *his* affectionate appeals; beside him was the tablet before alluded to, containing the record of *his* worth, who, "being dead, yet speaketh." If at one time more than another a minister feels the importance of his work, and the reality of eternal things, it is when he addresses his fellow-sinners as from the graves of the departed.

Alfred has since completed his eleventh year in Ireland. They have been years fraught with much mercy, as well as peculiar interest. It is to the singular and ample fulfilment of his youthful wishes the young reader's attention is specially called. This has been the one end and aim of this little volume. "TRY" never would have been written, but from the desire to *fix this thought*. The writer wants every boy to rise from its perusal, thinking of the particular end and object which *he* may have at heart, and which he may feel to be a lawful one, "Well, I will TRY, too." Not "I cannot;" not "It is of no use;" but "With God's help, I will TRY—I will TRY."

Through God's goodness and mercy—all the praise is due to Him, and Him alone—John *tried*, and Alfred *tried*. John had what he *tried* for, and so had Alfred. John wanted to preach and write; he did preach and write too. Alfred wished to be a parochial minister—to write and to print; and God gave him what he wanted. With the foregoing simple facts before him, the young reader need not, therefore, be dismayed at difficulties, nor discouraged by improbabilities. Be it his mercy first to ask God to be his Guardian and Friend, and then, with respect to the attainment of the things of this life, in so far as they are lawful and right, resolve to

TRY.

END OF PART I.

TRY AGAIN.

PART II.

INTRODUCTION.

IN this Second Part of the work it will be seen that the author has written in a deeper and more advanced style. It is hoped that his young readers will not object to this. They would not like always to continue as they are—*young;* they would not choose to remain unoccupied, and not to be called to fill any post in society. There is something in our common nature that aspires to *advancement.* Its language is, *Onward! Onward!* The child wants to become a youth; the youth, a young man; the young man, a father; and, as a father, and in an advanced state of manhood, he is anxious to fill at least some position which shall prove him to be a useful, a respectable, and a respected member of society. Now this is the very feeling that this book seeks to inculcate. It has been written for the express purpose of stimulating and encouraging. Its password is TRY, and TRY AGAIN.

It will, probably, interest the young reader to know, that this new edition has been prepared under circumstances most grateful to the writer's heart. By reference to the preface of the second edition, it will be seen that mention is made of two youths—the one as just being raised from a bed of sickness: he is now grown up to manhood, and filling a respectable situation in a banking-house. The other—the author's eldest son—at that time just entering upon his University course, having since pursued that course most successfully, was ordained by the beloved Bishop of Carlisle, and is now labouring as Incumbent of a parish, in a picturesque suburb of the city of Carlisle.

These facts, it is most earnestly hoped, will stimulate the young reader to diligence—to application—to resolve, under God, to

Try, and Try Again.

CHAPTER XXIX.

ALFRED'S CONTINUANCE IN IRELAND — FAMINE-SCENES — COTTAGE LECTURE—THE POOR FARMER AND HIS SIX SHEEP—REMARKABLE ANSWER TO PRAYER—CONTRIBUTIONS FROM ENGLAND—VISITS TO THE STARVING—TIMELY AID.

AS a new edition of this little work is called for, and as very considerable changes have taken place in the position of one whose name so often occurs in the foregoing pages, since the last edition was published, JONATHAN has resolved to introduce fresh matter under the above heading. At that time, as stated in the last chapter, Alfred had completed his eleventh year in Ireland. Now, for the sake of the connexion, and in order to render this little work more complete, it will be necessary to give an outline of his course in the sister-isle, and some few particulars of what has happened since the commencement of the issue of the last edition of this book.

It has already been stated, that, by a singular train of circumstances, in which the leading and sustaining hand of God was most marked, Alfred was invited to Ireland. He had been previously introduced to a most zealous and godly Bishop by an old correspondent of the periodical referred to in page 163, and was led on that occasion to express to the kind-hearted prelate what had

been his prevailing desire for many years with respect to the Ministry of the Church of England. The result was an invitation to Ireland. This happening at the close of the year 1846, when the famine was so fearfully raging, opened up at once a wide field of usefulness. As one of the links of divine Providence, so directly connecting present with after-circumstances, it may be *mentioned* that the stepping-stone (so to call it) was this. Within a month of his arrival in Ireland, and entrance upon his work of cottage lecturing, as preparatory to the Ministry, Alfred was one day walking out of the town of Templemore, where he was located, to a small farm-house at the foot of the neighbouring mountains. He mused, as he walked, upon Christ as the Good Shepherd, intending to make *that* the subject of his lecture. Upon his arrival at the farm, he found the inmates in great trouble. Their little flock of six

sheep, which they had been tending with great care, and with the produce of which they had intended to pay their rent, had been stolen the night previously. The poor farmer had left his bed two and three times a-night, to see that they were safe. He had even done so upon the night on which they were taken. This circumstance naturally suggested an illustration in regard to the Shepherd and His sheep. He (the Good Shepherd) never loses one of *His* sheep, for He says, "I give unto my sheep eternal life, and they shall never perish; neither shall any man pluck them out of my hand." At the close of the little service, the troubled family were commended to the care of God; He was asked to sanctify the loss, and, if it were His will, to restore the sheep. It certainly seemed an unreasonable request, inasmuch as in those dreadful times, and in the midst, as that little farm-house was, of the dreaded Tipperary, such a restoration was most unlikely, for both sheep and oxen had been stolen all round the neighbourhood.

Upon his return to his lodging, Alfred wrote to a dear friend in England, to tell of the loss of the poor farmer, as well as of other most distressing scenes which had come under his notice. The result was a contribution, by return of post, of a cheque for £15, to be distributed to the best of his judgment. Meanwhile (singular to say) the sheep were recovered. Daylight overtook the thief some six miles away, and he, fearing detection, ran off, and left the sheep. It was a most unheard-of circumstance in that part of the country, and in those times, when carts were so constantly stopped on the road, and robbed of their contents, that at length it became necessary for provisions to have an escort of soldiers as a protection. And thus for months were the meal and flour carried through the country.

Commencing with the sum above-mentioned, Alfred and the curate of the parish went from cabin to cabin, relieving the various cases with a ticket for half-a-stone of common Indian meal. Inquiries were made into each case; the name, the number of the family, and their means (if any) were noted down, together with any special fact connected with the various cases.

In proof that small beginnings ought never to be despised, it may be mentioned, that, when this little daily record was commenced, it was not with the least idea of its being published. It was merely written for the satisfaction of the kind friend who had forwarded the money. But, when the said little record was read to a second person, she suggested that it should be printed in the magazine before alluded to. The interest of its readers was thereby so aroused, that a sum amounting to nearly £700 was, in consequence, forwarded to the editor, by which immense relief was afforded to a very large district, and, to use the words of some of the poor Irish themselves, hundreds were rescued from death.

With respect to that visitation of divine Providence, it may be said that most marked and painful was the change brought by the failure of the once staple food of the country. Before, if you visited the Irish cabin, you might see its occupants grouped round a huge pot, well supplied with potatoes, from which they would liberally help themselves, whilst the pigs and the poultry as freely partook of their share. But now all was dark and drear. Desolate was the scene without, when the autumnal blast and the wintry frost had stripped the trees of their foliage, and snow covered both field and meadow, hedge-row and cottage-thatch; but far more

gloomy was the scene within, where neither food nor fuel were to be found, but where famine, in all its gloom and horror, reigned. Much, indeed, might be said upon this subject, but the theme is too sad to dwell upon. Detail would only harrow up the reader's feelings too painfully. Enough has been said to show the kind and gracious interest which God condescends to take in His creatures, as well as to connect the links in the chain of Providence by which Alfred was led.

CHAPTER XXX.

ALFRED'S APPOINTMENT TO THE CURACY OF MONKSLAND, BONMAHON —DESCRIPTION OF THE VILLAGE—TRAMORE BAY—THE POOR MARINER—HIS CLAIMS—COAST SCENERY—MAN'S GUILTY CONDITION—DIVINE FORBEARANCE.

AFTER his ordination, Alfred was appointed to the sole charge of a parish upon the sea-coast of the county of Waterford. Here is the village of Knockmahon, with the little church, and a row of miners' cottages contiguous. Connected with the district were large copper-mines, which in some parts ran to a considerable depth, and extended far out under the sea. Alfred's entrance upon this his new sphere of labour, and description of the place, will be best expressed in his own words :—

The village of Bonmahon has been deemed of so little importance as only occasionally to find its way into ordinary maps of Ireland. By reference, however, to the Ordnance map, and to some few others, it will be found upon the south-west coast of the county of

KNOCKMAHON.

Waterford. The Bay of Tramore lies ten miles to the east, and that of Dungarvan the same distance to the west. From the peculiar inset of the current, a vessel keeping too close to the land, upon a lee-shore, can seldom get clear of Tramore Bay. A transport was lost there, with most, if not all hands, when returning with troops from the battle of Waterloo, and numberless vessels since. To gaze upon these cliffs on such a day as when the accompanying sketches were taken, would afford the reader but a faint idea of their aspect in a storm. Under a south-west gale the sea will dash with fearful fury on their base, and throw the angry foam far o'er their brow. Often has the writer seen this shore, which now, and in these sketches, looks placid as a lake, lashed with such fury that the strand has been perfectly unapproachable; every house in the village has been covered with the surf, looking in the distance as though there had been a dense fall of snow. Perhaps nothing is more calculated to awaken sympathy for mariners than the residing on such a coast. How often does one retire to one's bed on a winter's night with deep emotion, as one listens to the howling of the tempest, and the roar (as it has been termed) of "the eternal wave." The thought of the multitude that are tossed upon the tempestuous deep, and the many that ere the morning dawn may find a watery grave, inspires one with gratitude for one's-self, and deep solicitude for others. The subject may well suggest to the reader cause for thanksgiving, if his lot be otherwise cast, for assuredly the sailor, braving as he does from year to year the mighty ocean, and deprived of advantages for social improvement, as well as foregoing countless comforts, is of all men entitled to our commiseration. The writer would impress these thoughts upon the young especially. These cabins form part of the village of Bonmahon, which is simply separated from that of Knockmahon by a small river called the Mahon, that comes winding down the valley from the Comragh mountains (some ten miles away), and finally emptying itself into the St. George's Channel at the Bonmahon

BONMAHON.

strand. Knockmahon is an Irish word, and (the village being built upon rising ground) it means the *hill* of the river. Bonmahon (built in the valley) implies *heel* or *foot* of the river.

The district is almost exclusively devoted to mining purposes. The Knockmahon mines are in great repute for the amount of copper they produce. But apart from its contiguity to the sea, and beautiful cliff scenery, the village in itself is as poor as can well be conceived.

The Bonmahon cliffs are extremely bold, and present an almost infinite variety. The annexed sketch is taken from the western end of the strand. The view in the preceding page is within a few hundred yards to the right. Let the reader take a map, and imagine himself standing on Helvic Head, looking eastward; he then has one of the most lovely panoramic views that ever feasted the eye. To the left of the spectator is the beautiful Bay of Dungarvan. Rising in a semicircle from the shore is a lovely landscape. To the left it stretches far and wide towards the flourishing town of Clonmel, in the county of Tipperary; the western limit of the Comragh mountains forms the central background; and to the right the view is bounded by the ocean, which flows at the base of a range of cliffs scarcely to be exceeded for grandeur and variety. Branching far out into the sea, as does the promontory upon which the reader is supposed to be standing, and forming, as was said, the outer curve of a semicircle, the spectator has brought very much before him some forty miles of coast scenery, the Saltee Islands being within view. It appears as though he were gliding along on shipboard on a lovely summer's day, and contemplating enthusiastically the ever-changing aspect. It would exceed our limits, otherwise it would afford us much pleasure to give a sketch from this spot, for we can scarcely conceive of any coast scenery more beautiful.

A multitude of thoughts crowd in upon the mind as one stands gazing on this enchanting scene. The ocean spreads itself into the far distance, without the veriest

BONMAHON CLIFFS.

interruption; there is a hallowed silence; not a note breaks upon the ear, except that of the scarcely-perceptible ripple at the base of the cliff upon the brow of which one stands. Upon the far-off waters is the snow-white sail, and the out or home-bound bark. Who and what are they thus borne upon the bosom of the mighty deep? Sinless are the occupants of yonder craft as thus they commit themselves to the oft-tempestuous ocean? Nay, but poor fallen, sinful, and ever-sinning man is he who glides upon the surface of an element to which, but for divine guardianship and care, he might presently fall a prey. One shudders at the thought of how the great Creator is defied, how His hallowed name blasphemed, even at the moment when so much above —around—show forth His power and handiwork. Oh, sin, what hast thou done? And how marvellous the divine forbearance with respect to those "that go down to the sea in ships, that do business in great waters; who see the works of the Lord, and His wonders in the deep." But, looking landward, is the state of the case, in this respect, improved? Are there here no proofs of sin? See how all nature smiles, as if in lively response to Him who at first declared it "to be very good." What can be more perfectly enrapturing than that vast and beauteous scene which is now laid before one? What is there to interrupt the seeming harmony that so universally prevails? Ah, come with us, reader, and speedily shall you see how God's creation has been marred by *sin*. Behold this village, beautifully circumstanced as it is; see its wretchedness and misery, mark the haggard, dejected countenances of its inhabitants, and then admit the contrast!

CHAPTER XXXI.

ALFRED'S FIRST IMPRESSIONS WHEN ENTERING UPON HIS CURACY—IRISH PEASANTRY—ROMISH PREJUDICES—THE IRISH PEASANT'S NEED OF BETTER INSTRUCTORS—THE FAMINE A BLESSING.

SUCH thoughts passed the writer's mind when first he entered the village where his lot was cast for upwards of ten years. His first conclusions were, that nothing could reconcile him to such an unseemly spot. Let the reader turn to the sketch of Bonmahon; and, excluding from his mind all idea of its position, let him conceive of a hundred or a hundred and fifty such cabins as those represented, occupied by say a thousand inhabitants; and these for the most part cradled in ignorance, superstition, and the most inveterate hatred of everything English or Protestant. Taught from very babyhood to believe that all their ailments arise, not from any radical defect in their own system, but solely as the result of English misrule and Protestant oppression, the difficulty of combating the deep-seated prejudices of the Roman Catholic peasantry in Ireland none can imagine but those who have tried the experiment. Introduced as their religion is into the every-day transactions of life, every effort for their mere temporal instruction and advantage awakens their suspicion; and, because such efforts may be those of a Protestant or of an Englishman, enmity is aroused, and opposition offered. One must "live, move, and have their being" in the midst of this suspicion, enmity, and opposition, to know what it involves. Years must pass over, and a ceaseless spending and being spent in the labour of love must mark one's career, ere any visible impression can be made upon minds thus constituted.

Familiar as the writer was with the most heartrending and never-to-be-forgotten famine-scenes, and agonizing as those scenes were, they have left, notwithstanding, a pleasing recollection of the gratitude which he witnessed on the part of the peasantry. There is a warmth and a heart about the so-called "Tipperary boys" that the writer admires. Unhesitatingly, he says they are worthy of better instructors, and, once freed from their crushing, tyrannizing hand, they would prove themselves to be what in reality they are—a noble people! The writer is one of those who believe the famine to have been among the greatest benefits that could have befallen Ireland. It was attended with a twofold good. It drew off the cotter from his hereditary and indolent dependence upon the potato crop, and it placed Protestantism before him in a light in which he was never wont to regard it. He saw the earnest, active, self-denying efforts of its ministers in relation to the poor and the perishing. By their instrumentality they were snatched, as it were, from the brink of the grave, and brought back again into life; and, in due time, their energies were directed into a new and prosperous channel.

The parish of Monksland is united to that of Abbey, or Innislonaghty, twenty-five miles distant. The rector, consequently, resides there, and the curate has sole charge of Monksland, Bonmahon. It was with a measure of reluctance the writer left the Tipperary scenes, notwithstanding all he had witnessed. He had not merely to encounter the weeping farewell of the once famine-stricken poor, but he had to bid adieu to his little mourning group upon the mountains, to whom he had been privileged to minister in such eventful times; from many warm friends, moreover, with whom he had been so closely associated amid those distressing scenes, he had also to be separated. His field of labour was now to be entirely changed. He was again a stranger in a strange land. Perhaps he may be allowed to state his feelings in the prospect, as elsewhere expressed*:—

My First Curacy.—Upon an early page is sketched our little church. 'Tis planted by the sea, and derives its name from being the site where monks, in former days, resorted. Peculiar was the interest it aroused when first I saw it. It was the evening of a day in autumn. Varied were my musings on a long and tedious journey, in connexion with the place, the people, and the prospects of my ministry among them. Reaching at length the summit of a lofty hill, the ocean opened to our view; and, just at that interesting moment, Jehovah spread His bow across the heavens: one end was planted far inland, the other dipped the waters. It spoke in silent, yet most powerful language —that, though strange and altogether new the course on which I was about to enter, the spot to which I journeyed lay there—beneath the bow of promise—and under the omniscient gaze of that Almighty One who had entered into covenant with each and every object of redeeming love, saying, "I will be with thee, and will keep thee in all places whither thou goest; and will not leave thee until I have done that which I have spoken to thee of." Sweet, therefore, were the respondings of my heart—

"Thou Author and Ground of my hope,
Thee, Thee for my God I avow;
My glad Ebenezer set up,
And own Thou hast helped me till now.

---

* See "Musings," by Alfred, page 218.

> "I muse on the years that are past,
> Wherein my defence Thou hast prov'd,
> Nor wilt Thou abandon at last
> A sinner so signally lov'd."

Such were one's emotions, spiritually, at one's first approach to this neighbourhood; but these having in measure subsided, one's heart perfectly sickened in walking through the village itself, and beholding the filth, and the wretchedness, and the misery that presented itself on every hand. It seemed unendurable. One felt as though one could never settle down in the midst of so much that was so exceedingly depressing. It had been said by the Bishop of Cashel, in his first conversation with the writer upon the subject of Ireland, that "it needed a missionary spirit; that there was nothing to be found in Ireland pleasing to flesh and blood." The "missionary spirit" was, under the circumstances mentioned, put to a severe test. The writer has a vivid recollection even at this distant moment of the sinking of heart this scene produced, to say nothing of the meeting of a strange congregation—the majority Wesleyan Methodists.

CHAPTER XXXII.

WISH TO ESTABLISH AN INDUSTRIAL PRINTING-SCHOOL—PROPOSITION TO REPUBLISH "DR. GILL'S COMMENTARY ON THE BIBLE"—DIFFICULTIES SURMOUNTED—MAGNITUDE OF THE UNDERTAKING—DEATH OF A DEAR FRIEND—UNEXPECTED LEGACY—PROGRESS OF THE WORK—INCIDENT ABOUT A BOY AND HIS AFTER-SUCCESS.

TIME, however, rolled on; the strangeness subsided; one gradually became inured, but never reconciled, to the sadly-neglected condition of the people, and more especially the young, of the village. Connected with his own little church, which may be seen in the first cut, standing near the brow of the hill, was a parochial school; but the elder boys of that school were growing up without the slightest prospect of occupation. The writer felt this, both on their own account, and on that of their parents. An idea had long presented itself to his mind—suggested first by a similar institution in the east end of London—it was that of a printing-school in connexion with a parochial school. The writer was engaged in editing the *Gospel Magazine*, whilst the printing and publishing of it were carried on in London. At length an opportunity offered for accomplishing his long-cherished desire. He had secured, through the medium of the periodical aforementioned, a number of subscribers to "Dr. Gill's Commentary on the Bible." He had proposed to publish an abridgment of this voluminous work for the sum of three guineas. At this juncture a gentleman offered to take *one hundred copies* at that price, provided the work were printed entire; but, when informed of the projector's intention to endeavour to set up a printing-school, and to issue it thence, he wrote to say he had no confidence in the undertaking; that it ought to be done by a person of large capital, and in London; that consequently he must withdraw his name as a subscriber, and have nothing to do with the work.* So large a number of copies being declined, was most discouraging. However, the mind being bent upon the work, one went forward. The writer having first made out a draft or scale of the cases in which the types are deposited, placed it in his schoolmaster's hands, and said, "Now let the elder boys take copies of this, and make themselves masters of it against my return." He then started for London; and, after considerable demurring on the part of the publisher, who was to receive all, and

* This gentleman afterwards duly fulfilled his engagement; and has also largely subscribed to subsequent works.

to pay all, at a certain per centage, the types, presses, and general materials of a printing-office were purchased. One friend spoke of it as "a perilous undertaking;" another said, "The establishment will be destroyed;" the publisher said, "Boys, you know, are of no use for the first six months." "I know the character of the boys I have to do with," was the reply. Three compositors and one pressman were engaged; and, in a few days, the writer once more found himself in the village, with these young men, and a large quantity of material, but no place in which to commence operations. A house, for the rental of which the negotiations were considered as closed, was refused; a barn attached to the cottage he had long occupied at an extravagant rent, was also refused, under the idea that the enterprize was to be turned to proselytizing purposes. The materials were scarcely landed at Waterford Quay before the Romish press opened its deadly fire upon the work. Still the watchword was "Forward!" There was no retracing one's steps. We were under engagement to produce the work by a given time, despite all difficulties. Happily, and as the providence of God graciously ordered it, a house which had been built for an hotel was available (a sketch of which is given on the opposite page). Then it was let to separate families. These gave place to the incoming tenant; and, within eight-and-forty hours of the arrival of the materials, operations were commenced. The boys were introduced, and their knowledge of the cases, by means of the draft before spoken of, put to the test. To the writer's astonishment, no sooner were the various pages of the new and dazzling type unpapered, than the boys began to distribute them into their varied compartments with an avidity and an interest for which he was not at all prepared. On Wednesday morning, October 15, 1851, the first portion of copy was given out. It was an herculean task in prospect. The principal actors were complete

novices. They had never seen type nor press before; and here by a given date—rather more than two years—this large work was to be reprinted, under the greatest possible disadvantages.

But for a desire to encourage and to stimulate others in efforts for the well-being of their fellow-creatures, the writer would not intrude upon the reader with any remarks about his own state of mind in relation to this great undertaking. This little work may, however, fall into hands that need to be upheld. There may be many a philanthropic heart throbbing with an intensity of desire to be of service to fellow-mortals; its possessor at the same time hesitates to enter upon an attempt at fulfilment of long and ardently cherished desires. Fear (so natural to man) may be construed into a providential negative, instead of a preservative from rashness, and a constantly-stimulating motive to prayer. Let us, then, take the Bonmahon work as a test how far good may operate, in spite of the difficulties and discouragements with which an undertaking may be encumbered, and the fears of a failure which may more or less prevail.

Now that the primary object is achieved, the whole may appear smooth and easily practicable; but could the reader have inspected matters in their infancy—could he have witnessed the initiatory detail—how different his conclusions! Let the reader consider—1. The enterprise involved an outlay of several thousand pounds; 2. It was to be accomplished in an obscure and most inconvenient village, upwards of 400 miles from London, where all the materials had to be procured, and to which the whole of the work when completed was to be forwarded; 3. The immense delay in supplying each fresh-discovered want in the numberless requirements of a printing-office; 4. The humidity of the atmosphere, which at times threatened completely to frustrate one's utmost endeavours; 5. The want of practical knowledge on the part of the majority engaged upon the work; 6. The determined opposition of the priesthood and its votaries;

7. The lack of public confidence; many a bookseller discouraged a proposing subscriber: "The work will never he completed," was the frequent exclamation; and some said, when it was even far advanced, that the work had actually been *discontinued;* lastly, The magnitude of the undertaking. When one saw arranged upon one's bookshelves NINE THICK QUARTO VOLUMES, containing *nearly forty-seven million separate letters,* and requiring *upwards of twenty-five tons of paper,* comprising above *eight hundred thousand large sheets;* and the whole responsibility for the accurate and workmanlike execution of which devolving simply and exclusively upon a humble village curate—with his varied ministerial and editorial duties in addition to perform—it did appear (when fairly begun) as though he had undertaken an impossibility! At times he felt overwhelmed, and reproached himself greatly for his sanguine folly. Prayer —deep and earnest—was his only resource. None but the great Searcher of hearts knew the oft-anguish of the writer's spirit, and the ardent pleading at the throne of grace for strength, courage, and perseverance.

And here he would pause to testify of the astounding goodness of his God. He had just said to a dear Christian friend, under the deep solicitude and burden of his soul, "Well, it's all in *the Lord's* hands," when a letter came; Miss Mary Anne Way (a personal friend and beloved correspondent of the *Gospel Magazine*) had died, and left him, in the most unexpected way, ONE THOUSAND POUNDS! The fact was published anonymously in a Bath paper; it went immediately the round of the press as one of several munificent bequests to clergymen; the Irish enterprize was mentioned also, and increased publicity given, and confidence secured; a large number of additional subscribers' names were returned; and the projector, thus relieved from the pecuniary weight of the undertaking, pursued his onward course with still greater zest. The consequence was, that within the first six months, instead of the boys (as had been intimated) being of no service, they had "composed," or put together, the types from which the whole of the first volume of the New Testament, comprising upwards of one thousand pages, were printed. Thus, *in their first half-year,* this little Irish group (utterly unacquainted as they had previously been with either type or press), had collected, or "composed," and arranged upwards of *eight millions of letters.* From the fifth week of their entrance they received wages, so much for every thousand types. Their application and perseverance were most gratifying. Often has the writer stood and gazed upon them with tearful eye and deep heartfelt emotion, as he has contemplated the activity of their movements, and their greatly-improved appearance! Our printing-school group, as taken in 1855 by photography, forms the next subject for illustration. However correct the outline and attire, the artist has failed to preserve the several likenesses. This would be almost impracticable in a woodcut.

A little incident about one boy in the establishment

may not be uninteresting. He had been admitted by the superintendent without, as usual, consulting the writer. His appearance was such, that the latter thought him too great a discredit to the place, and was about to tell him he could not be allowed to continue, when the boy approached him with a "composing-

stick" in his hand, and asked him if what he had done was correct. Upon looking at the lines, he found that they happened to be Dr. Gill's comments upon the 17th and 18th verses of the 16th chapter of St. Matthew, and these had been so correctly composed by this little Romanist that the writer was resolved for the present to forego his intention of excluding him on account of his ragged appearance. He remained—continued to improve—and is now filling a respectable situation in Liverpool.

The Commentary was finished within two or three weeks of the proposed time—viz., January, 1853. 2,250 sets of six volumes each were printed, numbering in the aggregate 13,500 volumes. As has been stated, upwards of twenty-five tons of paper were used on the work. The cost of carriage alone amounted to more than £300. The boys' earnings varied according to merit, from three to twelve shillings a-week. The Commentary itself was followed by 2,500 copies of Dr. Gill's "122 Sermons upon the Canticles;" 5,000 copies of Dr. Hawker's "Morning and Evening Portions;" 3,000 of a scarce and valuable work, Rev. Benjamin Keach's "Key to Open Scripture Metaphors;" 1,000 copies of Hart's "Hymns;" 2,000 copies of Ambrose Serle's "Church of God," to which is added his beautiful work on "Christian Husbandry;" 2,500 copies of Dr. Gill's "Cause of God and Truth;" 2,250 "Heart-Sighs and Heart-Songs;" 1,000 "Pathway of Providence," by the late Elizabeth Searle; Dr. Hawker's "Sermons and Tracts," 2,000 each; 7,000 of "Try," an illustrated book for boys; 2,500 "Keach on the Parables;" 2,000 Rutherford's "Letters;" 1,000 "Christ on the Cross;" 750 "Daily Meditations on Scripture." The *Gospel Magazine* was printed at the establishment for between four and five years; and the monthly penny pictorial broadsheet, *Old Jonathan,* was commenced in this industrial school.

Annexed is a sketch of the composing-room.

Perhaps no better proof could be given of the progress of that self-esteem which it is so desirable to inculcate in the minds of the peasantry of Ireland, than a fact connected with the annexed sketch. Neither

this engraving nor that of the agricultural school, as shown in another page, was taken by the photographic process. The boys, therefore, thought that the artist had not done justice to their present appearance; and some of them seemed to disbelieve, that, when first taken into the printing-school, they were shoeless, and tattered, and torn.

CHAPTER XXXIII.

FRESH WANTS—THOUGHTS OF AN INFANT-SCHOOL—ERECTION OF A BUILDING—OPPOSITION OF THE PRIESTHOOD—ALTAR DENUNCIATIONS—WRITER'S ADDRESS TO THE VILLAGERS—SCHOOL-TREAT.

HE writer having thus given an outline of the origin and progress of the printing-school, he would proceed to speak of another want which he had long felt to exist in the parish. The number of poor, half-clad, and sadly-neglected little ones that ran about the village, or crouched in or near their comfortless cabins, tended *deeply* to depress the writer's mind.

Annexed is a representation of a boy taken just as he appeared, and who was by no means the worst specimen that could be found. No remark was made about his dress; but he was taken by photography precisely as he was wont to appear. Contemplate such a condition. Imagine a large proportion, more particularly of the young of the village, in this state. It was most distressing. The writer felt it deeply. He wanted to rescue them from their misery. He would save them, if possible, from the natural consequences of such neglect. Hence he resolved to make the attempt to open an infant-school.

The village itself not affording the slightest accommodation for anything of the kind, the wish involved the necessity for erecting a school-house. Accordingly, in August, 1852, the building (70 feet in length and 20 feet in breadth) having been completed, the infant-school was opened. One plain meal of stirabout (or porridge) and skim-milk was allowed to each child per day. The writer felt justified in this course by the example of our blessed Lord, who "having compassion on the multitude, would not send them away empty." No undue influence was used. The parents were left to follow their own will.

This new effort exposed the writer to increased opposition on the part of the Romish priesthood. The altar rang, and the press teemed, with anathemas. The denunciations called forth an address to the inhabitants of the place, under date February 16, 1852. An extract from this document will perhaps be the best and readiest

way of putting before the reader the state of the case at the time the infant-school was in contemplation :—

You know there is an old and very good saying, "Hear both sides of the story;" and, as it appears that at first and second Mass yesterday, you heard your *priest's* side, I am sure you will be good enough now to hear *my* side.

And, first, I must tell you, that when Father Power called upon me on the 24th of October last, he said that, if our printing-school were not turned to proselytizing purposes, it would be a benefit to the neighbourhood. I said, in reply, that I had not intended, nor did I intend, to use any influence with the youth in my employ; but at the same time I remarked to him, as I now remark to you, that I long for the day *when every Irishman shall have his Bible!* It is his *right*, and I deeply grieve to see him deprived of that right.

Whether I have kept my promise with regard to the youth attending our printing-school, I must leave *you* to decide. Have I asked *one* to attend church? Have I *compelled one* to work on your saints'-days? Have I, in a single instance, said, "You must *turn*, or I cannot employ you?"—Christianity, not in name only, but in deed and in truth, teaches a man to *love his neighbour as himself.* In the spirit of that Christianity, I have done, and am doing, what I can do to help you. I felt for your distresses; I pitied the youth growing up to be burdens, instead of helps, to you; and I said to myself, "I'll try to assist them: I will teach them a trade; they shall earn money now, and by-and-by I will obtain them situations, where these once-neglected youths may become good and useful members of society. Moreover," said I, "I will prove to my countrymen—England shall know—that Irish men (aye, and Irish boys, too) both *can* work and *will* work, when they have work to do." To this end, as you know, I have spared neither trouble, nor toil, nor expense. At a cost of many hundred pounds I have set up my establishment, and having engaged sundry competent persons to assist me, have laboured both day and night to accomplish the great and important work I have undertaken.

Whether I have succeeded, the progress and the earnings of the boys will show.

But now in what have I given offence, and for what was I brought before you on the altar yesterday? Simply because I am asking English friends to help me to set up an infant-school. I have told *them*—and now I will tell *you*—that my heart bleeds when I see the poor, and the half-naked, and the all-but-starving little children running about our streets. I want to see them *clothed*, and I want to see them *fed*, and I want to see them *taught;* and, as your *priests* have not got up a school for them, *I* will try. And though I will not ask the children to become Protestants, nor will I ask them to attend our church—though I should be very glad to see either you or them there—yet this I tell you plainly, all that come to our infant-school will be taught to *read*, and taught to read the Bible too; and why? Because I cannot find, either in the Roman Catholic Bible, or in the Protestant Bible, any command to withhold this best of books—this choicest of all treasures—from the *poor* man any more than from the *rich* man. The *peasant* has as much right to the Bible as the *prince* or the *priest;* and you know the old saying, "What is good for the *priest* is good for the *people*."

The reader may smile at the children in the sketch being called "infants;" but, when admitted, it was found that they were as uninformed as infants. The sketch on page 177 will be recognized by many as that which appeared in the *Illustrated London News* for February 11, 1855, representing their usual annual feast, when seventy sat down to a good Christmas dinner of soup, beef, and plum-pudding. This scene was most animating. Many a contributor's heart would have been warmed could he have witnessed the improved health and appearance of the scholars, as well as have listened to their songs of praise, and progress in scriptural and general knowledge.

SCHOOL TREAT.

CHAPTER XXXIV.

PAROCHIAL AND INDUSTRIAL SCHOOLS—OCCUPATION ONE OF THE GRAND DESIDERATUMS FOR IRELAND—ITS ADVANTAGES AS A COUNTRY—RESPONSIBILITY CONNECTED WITH THE MAINTENANCE OF THE SCHOOLS.

THE elder boys are, from time to time, transferred from the infant to the parochial school. This school has been in existence for many years. In it the children receive a sound English education. At one o'clock they dine; after two the girls are instructed in plain needlework; and the boys adjourn to certain ground which has been laid out for an agricultural school.

Here, under the direction of the schoolmaster (who has a good practical knowledge of husbandry), the boys are put through a regular course of farm and garden labour, and have shown considerable aptitude, proving to a demonstration that there is no class more *willing* to work, nor any class more *able* to work, than are the Irish peasantry, under gentle and judicious direction. Left, as to too great an extent they have been, in a state of inertness, and wanting means of employment, it is astonishing with what willingness, activity, and perseverance they fall in with any scheme devised for their

AGRICULTURAL SCHOOL.

profit and advantage. Next to the Gospel, "Occupation" is the writer's watchword for Ireland. Under it he feels assured the whole aspect of the country would speedily be changed. Where is there a country with its genial soil and natural advantages, and where a people so remarkable for their endurance? Once break the fatal spell by which they are bound; once destroy the yoke that crushes them spiritless and heartbroken to the very earth; once give them to know and feel that they are verily members of God's intelligent creation—capable of thought, judgment, and discrimination—and not the mere tools or vassals of a mind-degrading and soul-destroying system; and then shall it be felt that indeed Ireland is

"Great, glorious, and free,
First flower of the earth, first gem of the sea."

The writer felt that, notwithstanding the provision for the boys and for the infants of the village, there was still employment lacking for the elder girls and young women. This led to the erection of a building exclusively for them. There was many a wanderer upon the cliff-brow, or lounger in the comfortless cabin, or the unseemly female labourer in the fields, who might be trained to work congenial with their sex. Despite priestly antagonism, this effort also proved most completely successful. In pleasing contrast to their former idle and destitute condition, they are comfortably clad, and earning an honest maintenance. Some who could not handle a needle, were afterwards engaged upon the most exquisite work, and received from four to seven shillings a-week.

The writer cannot bring his remarks to a close without stating, that he has been too great a dependent upon divine bounty to ascribe in any degree to himself the measure of success that has attended his humble endeavours. He can from his heart say, "Not unto us, O Lord, not unto us, but unto Thy name give glory, for Thy mercy, and for Thy truth's sake." Instrumentally, the writer's success is to be attributed solely to his long connexion with the *Gospel Magazine*, and to the generosity and very great indulgence of its readers.

EMBROIDERY SCHOOL.

Moreover, although much has been accomplished, much remains to be done. The projector's object is to give *permanency* to the system of industry and self-reliance it has been his privilege to introduce. In effecting this, he necessarily incurs an almost incalculable weight of care and responsibility. He stands as a lone individual, with but very slender personal means; he is connected with no society; nor has he any human instrumentality upon which to depend. As in the past, so now, the simple, yet indulgent and all-sufficient providence of God is that to which he can alone look, and upon which he can alone rely. Great was his responsibility at the time the Commentary was printing; his present responsibility is (if possible) greater. Then he had a sufficiency of subscribers to cover all expenses; now he has to find employment for his industrial band, and trust to Divine Providence to encourage persons to purchase the produce of the schools. His first great work not only met all expenses, but left a surplus; that surplus was laid out in the completion of a glebe-house, long wanting, in the parish of which the writer is curate. In consequence of the cheap rate at which the various works have since been published, the increase of the price of paper, and considerable advance in the cost of labour, *the printing school has not paid its way since the Commentary was completed.* As this establishment has from the first stood upon its own basis—the projector being solely responsible—the loss in question has fallen upon himself. He therefore appeals to the public to stand by him, and to stimulate him to further exertion by purchasing the works advertised in the last pages of this appeal. He trusts enough has been said in this simple, unvarnished detail, to prove that the really philanthropic mind cannot have a more desirable medium through which to gratify itself. By these industrial schools very many have been rescued from indolence, misery, and vice. Numbers who not very long since were to be seen loitering about, or lounging in their miserable cabins, are now diligently occupied from early morn to dewy eve in one or other of these industrial establishments. Nor are their minds allowed to run waste. Every legitimate means is offered for their improvement intellectually; and (though with the exception of the parochial, embroidery, and infant schools) the study of the Scriptures is not compulsory, yet there is a Sunday afternoon Bible-class, and week-day as well Sunday lectures, upon which some of the once unenlightened and prejudiced Romanists voluntarily attend.

It may be well to mention that this state of things cannot exist in a locality, more than nine-tenths Roman Catholic, without exciting the most determined and continuous opposition. To such an extent has this opposition been carried, that the doors of many a cabin (comfortless as those cabins are) have been closed against those who sought to earn an honest livelihood by means of these schools. A shelter from the weather, and a poor pallet of straw, has been considered too great a boon for such.

CHAPTER XXXV.

ANTAGONISM OF POPERY TO PROGRESS AND IMPROVEMENT—ITS DEADLY HOSTILITY TO PROTESTANTISM—AGED RECTOR—PROBABILITY OF THE WRITER'S REMOVAL AT HIS DEATH—THREATENING LETTERS.

FACTS in connexion with the foregoing will be gleaned from what the writer expressed in his Preface to the Third Edition of the pamphlet from which we have so largely quoted.

The following pages, he says, contain a simple, unvarnished statement of what, in the good providence of God, has been effected in a village where the writer has now spent nearly one-fourth of his life. At first sight of the place, he did not think of spending as many *months* as he has now spent *years*. But step by step has he been led on, until he has been privileged to see the most marked improvement in those with whom he has had more immediately to do.

Knowing full well the deep-rooted antagonism of Popery against Protestantism—especially against English Protestantism—the writer thought that instead of endeavouring to make converts in the common acceptation of the term, he would try to let his neighbours—almost exclusively Roman Catholic—see what *Christian* Protestantism was in operation. He uses the term *Christian* Protestantism, because he has very little sympathy with a lifeless, formal, merely nominal, and political Protestantism. Too many are making *it* a passport to heaven, ignorant of the fact that they are as far from the kingdom as their poor blinded Romanist neighbours.

In this spirit, and with much trembling of heart, he commenced his humble labours in this village; and, through the good hand of his God upon him, he has not been permitted to labour altogether in vain.

Much temporal good has been effected. Many that were in idleness have been for years occupied most diligently. Placed from the first upon a self-supporting principle, they have applied themselves to their work with an avidity, and pursued it with a perseverance, for which the writer was altogether unprepared when he commenced his labours among them.

The first school that he established in the year 1851 —namely, the printing school—is not only still in operation upon a somewhat extensive scale, but it is to his mind a gratifying fact, that the head of each department —that is the compositor's, machine or pressman's, and binding—was instructed in the establishment.

Sundry youths have been drafted off from the printing school, and are now filling respectable situations in England and America, as well as in Ireland.

The same habits of industry and self-reliance have been inculcated in the embroidery school. Where formerly there was a listlessness and a slovenliness, there is now a steady application, cleanliness of person, and altogether improved deportment. Many that owe their habits of self-dependence to this school, are now married.

As the children of the infant-school advance, they are placed either in the printing or embroidery schools, and thus carry into each school a good amount of Bible knowledge and general information. In the former, from the very nature of their occupation (the works printed being exclusively of a religious character) this knowledge is increased. In the latter school, every effort is made to inculcate Bible-truth.

From the agricultural school many of the boys have been transferred to farmers, having entered upon their duties as young agriculturists with a considerable amount of sound practical knowledge.

In his humble efforts to work a moral and radical improvement in this neighbourhood, the writer has endeavoured to put the simple truth before those with *whom* he has been more immediately connected; and left them to make their own conclusions, and draw their own inferences. He has had no wish to make converts (so-called) in name. He would prefer *one* leaving Romanism from thorough principle and sound conviction (and he believes he has at least one such) to a *hundred* from a half-heartedness, or selfish, impure motive. He has endeavoured to inoculate those within his reach with Bible-truth, and humbly and prayerfully leave the issue with his God.

Living in a Roman Catholic country, as one is called to do here, one's great aim, it appears, should be, to give heed to the injunction, "Inasmuch as in you lies, do good unto all men, especially unto those who are of the household of faith."

Facts, he believes, will prove that the writer has made no compromise with Rome. He has not the slightest sympathy with a system that has "gods many and lords many." He knows of but "one Mediator between God and man, the man Christ Jesus." He knows of none other name under heaven given among men whereby he or any poor fellow-sinner must be saved, but that of Jesus. "He, and He only, is made of God unto His people wisdom, and righteousness, and sanctification, and redemption; that whoso glorieth should glory not in the creature, but in the Lord." His principles upon this head are so well known, that, during the last year, he received no less than *six threatening letters*, declaring that his life should be taken: but his God has condescended so to make "the wrath of man to praise Him," as to render him perfectly indifferent to the malice of his enemies, and to cause him to understand practically the language of the Apostle when addressing the elders of Ephesus: "But none of these things move me, neither count I my life dear unto myself, so that I might finish my course with joy, and the ministry which I have received of the Lord Jesus, to testify the Gospel of the grace of God." Not with a proud boasting (God forbid!), but in the humble confidence of that faith for which he is indebted to the great Author and Finisher of faith, he can say, "For me to live is Christ, and to die is gain." "I am in a strait betwixt two, having a desire to depart, and to be with Christ, which is far better."

As regards the future, the writer is perfectly in the dark. If it pleases the Lord to prolong his life, he is willing to abide and labour here (although it is amid much that is exceedingly trying to flesh and blood) until He shall bid him strike his tent, and journey hither or thither. His rector is in his eighty-fifth year; his death will, most probably, be the signal for the writer's removal; but to what part of the vineyard is known alone to Him who "fixeth the bounds of our habitation." Seeing the nature of the work in which he has been engaged, this uncertainty was for years a source of pain and discomfort to him. He thanks God that He has given him relief upon this point. He is privileged now to have scarcely an anxious thought on the matter; *seeing* "our times are in His hand."

As long, therefore, beloved reader, as the writer continues here, he will (the Lord helping) ask your kind co-operation. Help him with your heart and hand to labour for the best of Masters, and in the noblest of all causes. "Let us work while it is called to-day, knowing the night cometh in which no man can work."

The writer feels called upon to add, that, should God, in His providence, remove him from his present sphere, and these establishments in consequence close, his labour will not have been in vain. The schools will have done their work. As stated in a previous page, they were commenced simply for the benefit of the boys of the parochial school, for whom, at that time, there was no human prospect whatever. The extension to others of the benefit which *they* have received, was purely an afterthought. However, not merely the youth of the parochial school, but very many others, have been so trained as not only to earn for themselves a present respectable livelihood, but have been qualified to fill —and many are filling—good situations. Many have grown up to man's estate, and have become useful members of society. Not only so, but a large amount of Bible-truth has been instilled; and—with thankfulness the writer would acknowledge it—he has seen the fruits of this teaching in sundry instances. Some, unquestionably, have been "turned from darkness to light, and from the power of Satan unto God." The writer is not generally sanguine with regard to conversion work, whatever he may be in other respects; but there are instances, as aforesaid, in which it would be sin in him, and the greatest ingratitude, if he were to call its reality in question.

Furthermore, such has been the universal change in Ireland, through the operation of the Encumbered Estates Bill, the great amount of emigration, and the number of English and Scotch settlers, that pauperism and want of occupation are now comparatively unknown. When the Bonmahon schools were commenced, the mines in the neighbourhood were almost at a stand, and labour was at a mere nominal value; the mines have long since revived, and the price of copper so advanced, that the labourer earns three times as much as formerly. Those, too, engaged in the printing school have fully trebled their earnings, when compared with the first year or two.

Another and most important fact is this; as stated in the annexed pages, the great work with which the schools were commenced, and (combined with the teaching of the boys) for which the printing school was established, was Dr. Gill's voluminous Commentary. For that a sufficient number of subscribers had *previously* been obtained to cover the cost; since which (as mentioned in page 182) the various works have had *first* to be produced, and *then* sold. This has subjected the writer to a considerable outlay, and a large stock being still both upon his and the publisher's hands, an immense weight and responsibility is the consequence. At times the writer feels this almost insupportable, seeing that *he* has to bear the burden apart from any local aid, or the support of any society. Perhaps the wisest course would have been at first to have placed the printing school, as the other schools were, upon a public footing;* and thus to have *secured a larger amount of public interest, and ensured a remunerative sale for the printed works;* but, at the time the printing school was commenced, there was such an entire want of confidence, and the whole scheme was considered so hazardous, that even the publisher himself hesitated to receive the first *entire* subscription to the Commentary which a humble servant-maid tendered, and insisted upon paying in full, saying she was confident the work would be completed. As it is, for want of a little consideration, many imagine that as the first work was productive, so of necessity must the after-works be; whereas *that* work was subscribed and paid for, and a large portion of the *latter* remains in stock; the former was printed at a much less cost, the latter (for the reasons before mentioned) have been produced at a much higher rate; intsead of

* True it is that almost every subscriber to the schools has left the application of his contributions entirely to the discretion of the writer; but in every instance (with the exception of £150, which was subscribed by a generous but unknown individual, and which was applied, by permission, to the erection of a new building for the printing school) it has been appropriated to the other schools. Not one pound has been applied to the printing school, the maintenance of which has been wholly upon the founder.

the general interest having been *increased*, the novelty having subsided, it has *lessened*; and the necessary consequence is, a much greater amount of care and responsibility upon the humble founder of these institutions.

CHAPTER XXXVI.

INDUSTRIAL SCHOOLS—LIABILITY OF ALFRED, THEIR FOUNDER, BECOMING INVOLVED—REFUSAL OF HIS LORDSHIP TO AFFORD HIM LEAVE OF ABSENCE—LETTER TO THE READERS OF THE "GOSPEL MAGAZINE."

FROM the last few pages it will be seen that, though the most gratifying results attended Alfred's efforts in the establishment and maintenance of his industrial schools from October 15, 1851, to February 17, 1858, the dates already given, still the responsibility was too great for *one individual.* The novelty had subsided; the first large work, published by subscription, was completed. Moreover—and here lay one of the chief difficulties—as there was no regular minister to supply his place when absent from the parish, Alfred's Bishop was unwilling that he should spend so much time in England each year, as it was absolutely necessary he should do, provided the schools were to be continued. Stock was accumulating; and, unless a market were found for it, the founder of the schools would soon become involved. This was foreseen, and hence a difficulty arose as to what was the right course to pursue. Other facts, likewise, led the writer to apprehend that his work was nearly completed in that part of the Lord's vineyard. Alfred's position and state of mind may be gathered from his own words, as given at the time and under the circumstances in question:—

TO THE READERS OF THE "GOSPEL MAGAZINE."

Beloved Readers,—As you may have gathered frequently from my observations of late, I have felt the cloud was moving from that sphere where I have so long been called to labour. Not merely in word, but in way, the Lord has been saying, "Ye have dwelt long enough in this mount; turn you, and take your journey." In spite of these indications, I had endeavoured in every possible way, and by every means, to "make my nest" where I was. Although from the first, and all through my career at Bonmahon, it was a most self-denying, and of late a most hazardous position, yet, on many accounts, I desired to continue there. There had sprung up a deep and mutual attachment between the people of my charge and myself. Eleven years is no small portion of one's life to dwell among a people. Cold indeed must be the heart that felt no special interest, but was indifferent, under such circumstances. Moreover, there was a retirement from the turmoil of the world that one liked, and there was the pure seabreeze and mountain blast, to brace one's nerves. There was the family-house, too, which one had taken an active part in raising. Last, but not least, there had been the felt presence of the Lord—the enjoyment of His power and smile in the ministration of the word. The realization of this, during the latter months of one's ministry among one's dear people, is perfectly indescribable. What I have felt, in the last nine months, when preaching on a Sunday and on Thursday evenings especially, and under the consciousness that each sentence might be my last,* is far beyond my power to express. Through the then present communications of my God—the pouring in, at the very moment, of light, and love, and blessedness—I have stood, in feeling and enjoyment, upon the very threshold of heaven. I have thought it not at all improbable that as I was one moment speaking *for* my Master, so it was extremely likely the next moment I should be speaking *to* Him. All fear of death, or dread of the ruthless hand of the assassin, was completely removed. I have stood "strong in the Lord, and in the power of His might." I write not thus in self-praise; God forbid: these matters are too sacred to be thus trifled with. I speak it in honour of my God, and in proof of what He is able to do, under the most trying circumstances. I wish, by my humble testimony, to encourage the mind of any that may have His work near at heart, and to say to them, upon the ground of my own personal experience, as well as His own precious testimony, "Fear not to go down to Egypt." No, my brother, if you can trace the

* This was in consequence of the threats of assassination—the pulpit being in a most exposed position, standing between two windows on the ground-floor, and most easily seen from the field, on the one hand, or the road, on the other.

moving of the cloud, and hear His gracious voice, saying, "This is the way, walk ye in it," you may, without hesitation, say,

"Cheerful where'er Thy hand shall lead,
The darkest paths I'll tread;
And joyful quit these mortal shores,
To mingle with the dead."

But, notwithstanding the facts to which I have alluded, I did, as before intimated, feel a strong and irresistible impression that my time was short among that people. Again and again did I tell them so. I used every means in my power to perpetuate my labours among them. I strove to the utmost to obtain subscribers for other works which it had been suggested to me to publish. I was comparatively regardless of the excessive wear and tear of mind and body which I was undergoing. Had my God made the way clear, I would have most cheerfully remained. The simple and sincere language of my heart was,

"Choose Thou the way, and then lead on."

"If Thy presence go not with me, carry us not up hence." But the Lord seemed, in the most significant way, to be closing the door, and to say, "Arise, and depart; this is not your rest."

As I have stated in the address to my late beloved parishioners, which I shall presently quote, on two occasions proposals had been made for an adjustment of the parishes, which would (in all human probability) have fixed me in Bonmahon for the remainder of my days. In the one instance, it was remarkable how many impediments had been overcome, and circumstances so dovetailed, as it were, that one said, "Surely this is the finger of God." However, just at the close of the arrangements, the Lord seemed as significantly to negative the whole matter; and from that time forward I had my doubts as to my very long remaining there. Humanly speaking, had I left it long since, it would have been better for me, in a temporal point of view; for, although my enemies say what I have done has been with a view to personal advantage, I can before God say, I have not only expended the proceeds of the work in the parish, but have also sacrificed nearly every shilling I had in the furtherance of that work. Personally I have expended considerably over a thousand pounds in the work at Bonmahon; and I now resign that curacy to begin life, as it were, afresh. This is my answer to my enemies. I have had petty jealousies to encounter, and innumerable suspicions to labour against. It has been said that so self-denying a work must be a profitable one. Let results prove. I feel thankful, that, in the closing up of my long and arduous labours, I can put my hand upon my heart and say, I have toiled for the good of others, and not for my own personal benefit.

By a reference to the extracts from the last edition of the "Outline of the Bonmahon Schools," it will be seen that both myself and the publisher have a large stock of books on hand. We have just completed the last volume—namely, a new edition of "Keach on the Metaphors," the order for which Mr. Collingridge gave me, not because the previous edition had sold out, but with a view to afford employment for the schools. To go on multiplying stock, merely for the sake of keeping up the schools, would seriously involve me. The apprehension of this has of late caused me many a sleepless hour, and tried my mind exceedingly. I therefore retire from the scene of my heavy and protracted labours, *whilst in a position to meet every demand.* I have borne the weight as long as it was possible to bear it. To have grappled with it longer would have made irreparable inroads upon my health, which has already suffered to a degree of which only the members of my own family are aware.

I leave Ireland with the consciousness that "I have done what I could" in her cause; and am abundantly recompensed by the reflection, that I have done it "as unto the Lord, and not unto men."

CHAPTER XXXVII.

CONTINUATION OF ADDRESS—THE PASTOR'S FAREWELL.

THE following letter was addressed to my late parishioners soon after my departure from among them :—

TO THE PARISHIONERS OF MONKSLAND AND BONMAHON.

My dear Friends,—Among the many ties which bind heart to heart, not the least endearing is that which exists between the pastor and his people. There are relationships which are of an exclusively natural kind, and friendships of a pleasing cast and abiding character; but, both the one and the other, death sooner or later must sever. The bond, however, which unites the spiritual pastor with a believing people is that over which the last enemy has no control. Theirs is an attachment so pure that nothing can sully it—so durable, that it shall outlive death, triumph over the grave, and flourish through the blissful ages of eternity. According to the length of time the pastor has abode with his people, and in proportion as the Lord has been pleased to bless his sojourn with, and ministrations among them, does he understand practically the language of the Apostle, "In Christ Jesus I have begotten you through the Gospel." He has his sons and daughters in the faith and hope of Christ, that are dearer to him than life itself; which shall be his joy and crown of rejoicing in the great day. As a father, the pastor watches, with a special and peculiar interest, the birth, growth, progress, and prosperity of his children. He is one with them. He "weeps with them that weep, and rejoices with those that do rejoice." But, pure as their attachment is, and lasting as is its character, there comes not unfrequently, in the providence of God, a season of sore trial—namely, the termination of the pastor's labours among his people.

For this trial in *our* case, my dear friends, I cannot think you altogether unprepared. This letter will not, I feel assured, take you by surprise. You cannot but have observed, for many months past, the bearing of my pulpit subjects. You have seen how deeply they were imbued with the idea of the changing, perishing nature of all things here. Nay, more; a moment's reflection will bring to your recollection seasons in which I have told you, in plain terms, that I felt an irresistible conviction that my time with you was *short*. The impression may be said to have originated some three or four years ago, when the proposed arrangement of the parishes was negatived just at the last juncture, and when so many singular coincidences seemed to have furthered an adjustment apparently so desirable. That negative appeared to me to be most significantly of God.

Had the proposed arrangement been carried out, it would most probably have fixed me with you for the residue of my days. The termination, however, of those negotiations, proved that "God's thoughts are not as our thoughts;" and, from that time forward, my mind has been unsettled. I, however, still laboured among you, and in that work to which the Lord had called me, in spite of my own feelings and impressions. I sought by every means to trace the footsteps of Divine Providence, and to ascertain the mind of God. Hence, when last year my venerable rector expressed his willingness to exchange his living for my small sinecure, in order to perpetuate my humble labours among you, I again made it a matter of earnest prayer before the Lord, that he would influence the hearts and direct the minds of those concerned. The subject of the exchange was brought before the late Lord Lieutenant, and, as you are aware, refused by his Excellency. This, again, I regarded as the finger of God. As the parish is in the gift of the Crown, and my rector has attained the great age of eighty-five years, with declining health, I deemed this a further indication that my labours were of necessity drawing to a close.

During my residence among you, I have endeavoured to leave myself in the Lord's hands. I trust I have been His willing and waiting servant. I have had, as you are aware, the claims of a large family, all of whom were dependent upon myself; and I think you will allow me to adopt the language of the Apostle, "I have coveted no man's silver, or gold, or apparel. Yea, ye yourselves know, that these hands have ministered to my necessities, and to those that were with me. I have showed you all things; how that so labouring ye ought to support the weak; and to remember the words of the

Lord Jesus, how He said, It is more blessed to give than to receive."

It is with no small amount of effort I am, at length, brought to the conclusion to leave Ireland, where I have passed little short of twelve years. Nearly one-fourth of my life has been devoted to her interests. Although my work has been fraught with intense anxiety, as well as heavy responsibility, I have had my reward in seeing many brought to the Lord, and in the unspeakable realization of divine comfort and consolation in proclaiming to you the unsearchable riches of Christ. I shall never be happier this side of heaven than I have often been in ministering to you.

To the thoughtless among you, I would affectionately repeat my frequent words of warning. Remember the solemn charge laid upon my heart, and with which I closed the services of the day the last Sabbath but two that I spent among you. I quoted (as you will remember) the words of a dying sister to her then thoughtless brother. "I charge you," said she, "to meet me at the right hand of God." (This she said, not denying man's total impotency both in will and power, but to give expression to the intensity of her dying concern with regard to eternal things. I have shown you, dear friends, how alone that can come to pass.) Whilst I have testified that there is "no other name given under heaven and among men, whereby we can be saved, but Jesus only," and have fearlessly and faithfully declared, "that it is not by works of righteousness which we have done, but according to His mercy He saved us, by the washing of regeneration, and renewing of the Holy Ghost," so have I proclaimed also the fulness and freeness of that salvation by the blood and righteousness of Jesus—a salvation "without money and without price." God, in mercy, grant you may be made partakers of the same.

To those among you who have obtained "like precious faith" with God's dear people, I would adopt the language of encouragement and exhortation—encouragement from consideration of the fact, that "now is our salvation nearer than when we believed;" exhortation, in the words of the Apostle, that last fell on our ears in Monksland Church, in our striking burial-service, the evening previous to my departure from amongst you, "Therefore, my beloved brethren, be ye steadfast, unmoveable, always abounding in the work of the Lord, forasmuch as ye know that your labour is not in vain in the Lord."

As to the Lord's work being retarded by my withdrawal, I am of opinion it will *help* the work rather than *hinder* it. Cavilling will now cease. The fact of my resigning will prove that the curacy of Bonmahon cannot be so advantageous as has been conceived. Relinquishing my post is worth a thousand arguments, for "facts are stubborn things."

Moreover, I resign under peculiar circumstances. I do not, as in most cases, surrender one post for the sake of entering immediately upon another, and that other generally an advanced position. Although, in years that are past, I had sundry spheres of labour offered me, of late such proposals have ceased. It was thought my connexion with Bonmahon was indissoluble. I leave it now in ignorance of where my future lot is to be cast. I am thankful, rather than otherwise, that it is so, believing that my God will provide. I doubt not He has a sphere of labour in waiting for me, though as yet I know not where that sphere is. Now that my mind with regard to Ireland is known, kind friends are interesting themselves in my behalf. The result is with my God.

One remark more, and I will close this somewhat lengthy address. Much as I should love to see you all again, my dear friends, and to minister once more "all the words of this life," I am compelled, from very necessity, to forego this sacred pleasure. I am not equal to it. I do assure you, my nervous system has been much taxed. The remembrance of the scenes of last year, when it was probable I should leave you, is too keen for me again to encounter them. I am not, dear brethren, prepared for a formal parting. It would unnerve *me*, and unnecessarily distress *you*. No; *this* will be the best mode of separating. I told you, at the grave of my late aged parishioner, on the day before I left, that *I thought I should never see you again*. I was afraid to trust myself to say more. I believed then, as I believe now, that our next meeting will be at the bar of God. Bear this in mind, my dear, dear people. The Lord the Spirit bring to your remembrance what He has helped me, for nearly eleven years, to set before you. I trust, however feeble my ministrations among you, and notwithstanding all the weakness and infirmity that has characterized them, that I may be permitted to say, "I have kept back nothing that was profitable unto you, but have showed you, and have taught you publicly, and from house to house, testifying repentance toward God, and faith toward our Lord Jesus Christ."

"And now, behold I know that ye all, among whom I have gone preaching the kingdom of God, shall see my face no more. Therefore, I take you to record, this day, that I am pure from the blood of all men. For I have not shunned to declare unto you all the counsel of *God*."

"And now, brethren, I commend you to God, and to the word of His grace, which is able to build you up, and to give you an inheritance among all them which are sanctified."

Brethren, farewell.

I am your affectionate Friend and Pastor,

* * *

Seymour Villa, Plymouth,
March 30th, 1858.

CHAPTER XXXVIII.

ADDRESS OF ALFRED'S PARISHIONERS TO THEIR LATE PASTOR—ALFRED'S REPLY.

FROM THE PARISHIONERS OF MONKSLAND TO THEIR BELOVED PASTOR.

WE would desire to express our deep and sincere regret at your leaving us; and how bitter has been the severing of those ties which have so long bound us together. For nearly eleven years you have faithfully ministered to us, and we will testify that you have "not shunned to declare unto us the whole counsel of God;" that your mission and labour of love, day and night, has been to exalt Christ Jesus above all things, directing and imploring all that were needy to come to Him—all that were weak and heavy-laden to come; warning the thoughtless, comforting the believer, speaking faithfully unto all, "that the name of the Lord might be glorified," fearless of taunt and scorn from the enemies of the Lord. You did, indeed, "weep with those that wept among us, and rejoiced with those that did rejoice." We believe that God has blessed, and will bless, the words which you have spoken amongst us, for He has promised "that His word shall not return unto Him void, but it shall accomplish that which He pleases." And we earnestly desire that the Holy Spirit would now bring to remembrance the lessons you have taught us, and abundantly bless the good seed sown in this place.

And now that it seems to be His will to withdraw you from us, we will, in the language of Job of old, say, "The Lord gave, and the Lord hath taken away, blessed be the name of the Lord;" and, though not permitted to conduct us further on our way homeward, heavenward, you have taught many here to know that the Lord our God will go with us, and will never leave us, never forsake us. The bond that unites souls in Jesus can never be broken; separation and death can have no power over that holy tie; and we trust the pastor and his people will be re-united at the right hand of God, washed and purified in the precious blood of Christ, where there will be no more parting, when all tears will be wiped away. It would be difficult indeed to forget the depth and sincerity of your affection, and your unquenchable zeal for God and His cause. And now, among the cares and labours of your new sphere, we trust you will never forget the little flock, the faithful hearts, you have left in Ireland. That every blessing of a covenant God in Christ may be with you, and that you and yours may enjoy the grace of God here, and rejoice in His glory for ever, is the heartfelt and affectionate prayer of your loving and sorrowing people.

[Here follows the signature of every Protestant parishioner, with the exception of four, one of whom wrote an affectionate private letter.]

REPLY.

My dear Friends,—I have long loved many of you in the Lord; but, until now, I knew not *how much* I loved you. I have often thought, and, as you know, spoken, of the love of Christ in His members, as well as to His own divine person. I never knew its reality so fully as I am called this day to experience it. Your most affectionate letter, just received, has opened, as it were, another vein in my heart, and from it flows, in warmth and tenderness, the sincerest affection and the intensest interest in and to you.

God bless you, my dear people.

We shall not—I feel *I* cannot—meet you again in this poor, perishing, sin-dyed world. *My* feelings—and I believe *yours* also—would be far too keen to encounter that formal parting of which I spoke in my previous address. Let it—God grant that it may—have the end of bringing us more earnestly and more frequently *to meet at His footstool.* Yes, we may meet there! In oneness of heart we can bow before the Father of mercies and the God of all consolation. No distance can prevent this.

Since I left you, I have ministered to many congregations, but I have not forgotten *you.* You have been, and will be, present in my remembrance, and embosomed in my heart, even though I may be proclaiming the unsearchable riches of Christ, and the sovereignty, efficiency, and durability of divine love, far, far away from you.

I rejoice, my dear people—for such I must still call

you—in your reference to the great work of the Holy Ghost. I would affectionately remind you of what I have often endeavoured to impress upon you, that it is His special prerogative "to bring to remembrance." Hence, in the exercise of His divine power, many of those great and glorious truths which it has been our meat and drink mutually to dwell upon, may be so brought to our recollection, as to afford abundant refreshing. To this end, dear people, *study the Word. Be much in prayer.* I hope it may please God that the prayer-meetings established among you may be continued. Prayer is a powerful lever. It moves the very heavens. Oh, have we not oftentimes felt its marvellous influence in our little assemblies?

Moreover, I would re-assure you of the great brevity of life. How soon will one and all of us have done with earth—how soon the place that now knows us will know us no more for ever. Soon, "He that shall come will come, and will not tarry." Each trial and every temptation will lessen those in reserve. If interested in Christ, we may cheerfully sing—notwithstanding all the dangers and distresses of the wilderness—

"A few more rolling suns at most,
Will land us safe on Canaan's coast;
Where we shall sing the song of grace,
And see our glorious Hiding-place."

Dear people, farewell!

Yours most affectionately in Christ Jesus,

* * *

70, Fleet Street, London,
20th April, 1858.

As this document will, I am sure, be preserved by very many who have been so much interested in my humble labours in Ireland, and who have so generously contributed to my work there, I cannot refrain from annexing the letters of my respected bishop and venerable rector.

Under date 9th April, the Bishop of Cashel writes :—

My dear Mr. ——,—Your most unexpected letter reached me this morning. It certainly startled me. I suppose you have fully considered the matter.

Your notice is very short, and your leaving rather abrupt, thus to drop everything at a moment.

A successor cannot be had in a moment. We trust, however, that the Lord will provide.

I am very sorry that the fears about your health should have led to this step which you have taken. I was not aware that your strength was giving way. I pray the Lord that it may be preserved, and that you may be able to serve the Lord in some other field of labour acceptably to Him, and comfortably to yourself.

I remain, faithfully yours,

ROBERT CASHEL, &c.

My aged and beloved rector wrote as follows, under date April 7, 1858 :—

My dear Sir,—You cannot conceive the distress your letter gave me, and all the friends to whom I mentioned the subject of it. Mr. L—— was quite distressed. It found me in my bed, and Sunday was the only Easter-day for forty-four years that I did not officiate in Abbey.

I have your letter resigning; it was written some time *last* May.

Miss H—— unites with me in sincere regrets, and also in the kindest regards to Mrs. ——.

Yours faithfully,

RICHARD MAUNSELL.

Again, under date April 17, my venerable rector writes :—

My dear Sir,—I received a very kind letter from the Bishop yesterday, in which he mentions that he will settle everything for me at Monksland. I imagine that he heard from some one that I had been so ill.

His Lordship seems to regret exceedingly your resignation, and with all who knew you and your exertions in the cause of our *Great Bishop*, the Lord of life, cannot but feel the irreparable loss the cause of God's truth will sustain where you seemed of such importance to His cause.

May the Lord, our heavenly Director, be with you and direct you in whatever sphere of duty you may undertake; and, believe me, you have no friend who will more sincerely rejoice to hear of your well-being than I shall, and whose sincere prayers will be offered up more frequently for you and yours.

Yours, very affectionately,

RICHARD MAUNSELL.

Thus ends my work in Ireland—fraught it has been with scenes both of pleasure and of pain. 1846 (the famine year) will never pass from my remembrance; nor will much that I have witnessed since. I have met with many dear brethren in the Lord in the sister isle, whose friendship I shall ever prize; others whom I was privileged to know and love, have "gone home." The thought of meeting both the one and the other—together with many (God grant, if it be His will, with all) of my dear parishioners, in that better land, is dear to my heart. I shall cherish the hope, and pray God for its fulfilment.

CHAPTER XXXIX.

SCRUPLES UPON THE PART OF MANY RESPECTING ALFRED'S LEAVING IRELAND—LETTER TO THE READERS OF THE "GOSPEL MAGAZINE" —ALFRED'S REFLECTIONS UPON LEAVING THE SCENE OF HIS PROTRACTED LABOURS—THE CLOSED DOOR IN PROVIDENCE— UNCERTAINTY AS TO THE FUTURE—HOPE IN THE PROMISES OF GOD.

THE many years which Alfred had spent in Ireland, and the deep and practical interest so long shown by his readers in his work there, led many subscribers of the *Gospel Magazine* to doubt whether he was right in the course he had taken. These fears were increased, because not only had he left Ireland without the prospect of an immediate engagement, and with a large family solely dependent upon him, but because several months elapsed without any permanent sphere of labour presenting itself. Hence, so far as *appearances* went, Alfred would seem to have taken a wrong step. The apprehension, therefore, of many of his readers led to the publication of the following in the work from which he has already quoted :—

Beloved Readers,—I have had many letters in reference to my recent unexpected change of position, and I purposed to say SOMETHING MORE ABOUT IRELAND, AND WHY I LEFT IT; but as yet documents and papers from which I must quote have not reached me, and therefore I must defer much that I have to say. Suffice it here to remark; that the more I reflect upon what seems to many to have been a *sudden* step, the more am I convinced that I could not have done otherwise, and the more I feel it was of the Lord.

One remark in my farewell letter to my late beloved parishioners, though perfectly understood by *them*, may need a word of explanation to *you*. In that letter, I alluded to my being utterly unable to encounter afresh the scenes of last year. I must tell you to what I there alluded.

After receiving the first threatening letter, I thought it might be an indication that it was the Lord's will I should leave, according to that scripture, "If they persecute you in one city, flee ye to another." Several of my parishioners besought me with tears immediately to depart, saying that they knew for certain evil was intended against me, and that my life was in the utmost peril. I said, "No, I'll not go alone; if I leave, my family shall go too." The pending examination of the suspected writer of the threatening letter having come off, and he having been discharged for want of proof, a large bonfire was made; I was carried about (as I was informed), and finally burnt, in effigy. But before the mob committed me to the flames, one of the most daring of them shot at the said figure. I heard (as I sat conversing with a dear fellow-labourer) a loud report. This proved to be the bursting of the blunderbuss, which, having been by some means *twice* charged, exploded, and blew off the top of the mock assassin's thumb. I saw the shattered weapon some time afterwards, and could but wonder that it had not blown off the delinquent's head; but, as it was, the loss of blood was so great, and the injury he had received so severe, that he was laid up in hospital for some two or three months. This circumstance was not without its use upon the easily-excited Irish character, and served in some degree to check their violence.

As long as the Lord clearly showed His hand, I was contented to remain. Whilst my heavenly Father was pleased to open His heart in and by instrumentalities altogether unsolicited, and which are known alone to Himself, I was willing to abide; but, when the brook began to dry up, and the Lord, in the clearest and most unmistakable way, said, "Thou hast compassed this mount, long enough; arise, and get thee eastward," "who was I, that I could withstand God?"

God forbid that I should be indifferent to the gracious dealings of His providence; God forbid that I, of all men, should ever be the mere creature of human policy. I may say, I have been a child of Providence from very infancy to this hour, and, moreover, I believe I shall be to the end of my days. My God has dealt with no niggardly hand towards me. If I have wanted a penny, He has given it; if a pound, I have had it; if a hundred, it has not been wanting; and if a thousand, even that thousand has been vouchsafed, blessed be His name! So that I, of all men, may speak well of Him. And I do so in praise of His name, and in gratitude to those many and kind instruments whose hearts and hands *He* has influenced, altogether without my solicitation. The timely, the tender, the gracious way in which my God has appeared for me, shall be my song in the house of my pilgrimage; and, when I reach home, I will praise Him in higher, nobler strains.

But mark, what my God has given has always been in *His* way, and in *His* time, not in *my* way, nor in *my* time. Moreover, the supply has been according to the *need*, not according to the *wants*.

From very necessity, I hope I have for many years simply acknowledged Him, and in earnestness and simplicity waited upon Him. I did so for years and years *before* I went to Ireland; I did so *in* going there; I did so whilst *abiding* there; and I trust with the same simplicity and teachableness, I sought the Lord with regard to *leaving* it.

But to return. I resigned the curacy; and, on the following Sabbath, after alluding, in a few words at the close of my sermon, to what I had felt it my duty to do, I left the pulpit. I was followed into the vestry by one of the churchwardens and the clerk, in tears. A third member of the congregation came in likewise, stating that the people would *not* disperse. The congregation remained in their pews for twenty minutes, precisely as I had left them, waiting for me to come out and discuss the matter. For this, of course, under the circumstances, I was unequal. I knew my feelings would give way, and therefore was compelled to decline it.

On the day following, however, a large meeting was convened without my knowledge, to which I, when all had assembled, was invited. They had collected together for the purpose of canvassing the whole matter. That weeping people I shall never forget. I could not encounter that scene again. I believe it would be my death. One, and another, and another, rose and spoke. The girls of the embroidery school said, "We will all become Protestants if you will stay," but I durst not act upon such a pretext. It was sincerity—it was voluntariness—I wanted in reference to a change of creed. It was *real* solid *principle* I looked for, and not mere *profession*. My enemies charged me with proselytism—in other words, with bribery. I throw back the charge; I disdained such a course. Had I pursued it, I could have made converts, so-called, by the score; but I challenge my enemies once again, as I have done numberless times before, to bring forward one solitary instance of either coercion or bribery during the whole course of my proceedings in Ireland. No, I sought by every fair, open, legitimate means, to teach and to train; but to disguised, underhand, jesuitical expedients I would never resort: for in doing so, I should only have copied examples which I was only too anxious in every way to avoid. Rome raises her noisy outcry about bribery and corruption, but it is upon the principle of the culprit himself crying, "Stop thief!" for it is notorious that there are none so guilty of bribery and corruption as is Rome.

But once more: at the meeting in question an argument was introduced which weighed much with me, and which I knew not how to answer. It was this, that if I left, it would be attributed to *fear*, and who would be able to stand their ground after that? "Stay, therefore, with us," said the people, "at least twelve months longer." Under these circumstances, I promised to reconsider the subject, and give them an answer that day week. Meanwhile, I received a letter from my venerable rector, expressive of the deep anguish my resignation had caused him, and urging me to come up and see him, in order to talk over the matter. I did so, and it was during that visit the subject of the exchange of his parish for my small sinecure was introduced. This was, in due course, brought before the Lord Lieutenant of Ireland, the Earl of Carlisle, but refused. This I naturally construed into another indication that it was not the Lord's pleasure that I should be a fixture in Ireland. It was the second time in which, in the most significant way, a negative was put upon what appeared *to be a* most desirable arrangement of the parishes, by which I should have been appointed permanently to Bonmahon.

At the adjourned meeting, I promised to remain in the parish until I could see more clearly the Lord's hand. I did so; and, almost immediately afterwards, I received the unexpected present of the £150, mentioned at the time. With this I erected the new printing school, and thereby gave my enemies proof that I was not to be frightened out of the village. I still watched closely the Lord's hand, and used every means in my power for procuring work for the schools. I was refused by my respected diocesan the time in England which was absolutely necessary for the collection of funds and disposal of work; and for months I saw, that, unless the Lord appeared in some remarkable way, I must close the establishment, or I should seriously and irrevocably involve myself.

The day before I left, a godly man, who had been with me for many years, came to me, and said, "Sir, do you think you will ever return to this place?" (I was leaving on a preaching tour the next day.) I said, "I don't know. Why do you ask?" "Because," said he, "I have been watching your discourses for a long time, and your mind has seemed imbued with the idea that your work is done here; *and I believe it is.*"

I left, and with considerable doubt upon my mind as to what was the Lord's will. A dear sister in the faith asked me, just as I was leaving, "Have you had a 'morning-word' to-day?" "Yes, but it has been taken from me again." I had left her but a few moments, and was driving out of the gate, through which it now seems I was never again to pass, when the word came with dew and power, "There shall be showers of blessing." I drove by those schools—through that village—by the church where I had for many years endeavoured to proclaim the unsearchable riches of Christ, and the churchyard where I had, on the previous afternoon, committed my senior parishioner to the silent grave, and addressed my poor Roman Catholic neighbours. I turned round and gazed upon those towering cliffs, where I had so frequently mused with feelings of mingled joy and sorrow; upon that beauteous shore, which I had so long delighted to contemplate amid the early rays of the rising sun, or the silvery beams of the midnight moon: I took a last and lingering look towards that far-spread sea, and asked myself, "And can it be that my work is *done?* shall I, so long familiar with these scenes, behold them no more *for ever?* have I, indeed, bade farewell to that loved people? shall the Gospel no longer teem from the press in this lone spot? shall the certain sound no longer be heard here?"

Thus I mused as I drove towards Waterford, on reaching which the funeral knell of the cathedral was tolling. Upon inquiry, I found it was for the departed wife of the Dean. I had just time, prior to the starting of the train, to follow that Christian lady to her last *resting*-place. In that cathedral where, a little less than eleven years before, I had received ordination, I listened to our solemn burial service: the last words which I had read in my own little church on the previous afternoon now dropped upon my ears again with strengthening, stimulating power: "Therefore, my beloved brethren, be ye steadfast, unmoveable, always abounding in the work of the Lord, forasmuch as ye know that your labour is not in vain in the Lord."

Thus ended, with me, the public worship of God in Ireland. On reaching Kingstown that evening, and going on board the steamer, *I was taken so exceedingly ill, that I was compelled to go on shore again.* My nerves were completely unstrung, and I suffered much the whole of the night. That night, and for days afterwards, I again spread my whole case before the Lord; the issue was—*a resolve not to return.*

I am perfectly satisfied that this determination was of the Lord, and the more I reflect upon the subject in all its points and bearings, the more convinced am I that I could not have come to any other conclusion; but, at the same time, it has caused me an amount of pain and anguish, mentally, which words cannot express, nor heart conceive. As I stated in my second letter to my late beloved parishioners, I could not have believed that the bond between pastor and people was nearly so close and endearing as I have since proved it to be.

I have had one source of relief since I left my dear people—and, seemingly, but one—and that is, the ministering to other congregations. My happiest moments have of late been in the pulpit. With few exceptions, each time I have been privileged to preach, it has been from the fulness of my heart, under the present realization of the power and presence of the Lord. But the moment of leaving the pulpit has been the signal for again taking up my burden.

It may be asked, "And what is the present state of your mind?" I answer, "Perfect ignorance of what the Lord intends to do with me, or where He means to place me." A few days before I left my Irish home, these words were forcibly impressed upon my heart: "Said I not unto thee, that if thou wouldest believe, thou shouldest see the glory of God?" From the power with which these words were applied, and from the manner in which they afterwards rested upon the mind, I felt that something was coming; but I little knew the full nature or real extent of the trial. The death upon the promise was never more absolute. The reality of trial was, perhaps, never keener; and yet, probably, there never was a clearer sense that I had the Burden-bearer at hand. There has been His felt power, and His felt presence. There has been a consciousness that but for this, the trial (more especially in its gloomy apprehensions and forbidding prospects) would have been far more severe. No; the Helper has been at hand. I dare not speak of my untowardness. I should blush to own the occasional hard thoughts—and the all-but outbreaking of hard words too—against my ever-gracious God, my patient, forbearing, long-suffering

Friend; and this, too, when there has been a thorough conviction that what He did must be right, and a heart-trembling at the veriest idea of being left to one's own choice, or to be allowed to have one's own way. How desperate is rebellion under these circumstances! How cruel to *think* unkindly of God, when one *knows* and *feels*, and dares not doubt for a moment, that wisdom, and love, and the utmost tenderness, move both His heart and hand!

Amid all these conflicting feelings, there is still the word resting upon the heart, though as yet altogether unfulfilled, and no knowledge whatever how, or when, or where it is to be opened and ratified,—"Said I not unto thee, that if thou wouldest believe, thou shouldest see the glory of God?"

CHAPTER XL.

ADDRESS OF THE PARISHIONERS OF MONKSLAND TO THE LORD BISHOP OF CASHEL — ALFRED'S LETTER TO HIS FORMER PARISHIONERS.

WHEN the schools had been broken up, and his family had returned to England, Alfred resolved to make the effort once more to visit the beloved people of his late charge. He, at the same time, made arrangements for sending several of those employed in the schools to Canada.

Shortly after his return to England, he received a copy of the following address to the Right Reverend the Lord Bishop of Cashel, &c., from the parishioners of Monksland, Bonmahon:—

We, the undersigned parishioners of Monksland, feel it a privilege and duty to bring before your Lordship, as the Bishop in whose charge God has placed us, some statement of the value and importance of the labours of our highly-esteemed and beloved pastor, the Rev. — ——. During the long period of eleven years he has been amongst us, doing his Master's work with a zeal and energy which has been owned and blessed of God. Some are now casting their crowns before the throne above, whose hearts have been made glad by his ministry here; others have gone to distant lands, and are there rejoicing in the knowledge of salvation as it is in Jesus, looking back to this humble village with love, as the place where that knowledge was obtained through the mercy and blessing of our God. Many are still sojourning here, bitterly lamenting the loss they have sustained of a sympathizing friend and faithful pastor; one who has not shunned, through many hindrances, to declare unto us the whole counsel of God. We feel that during the stay of such a one amongst us, we were a people highly blest and favoured of God, and still we trust in Him that many precious promises shall be fulfilled both to pastor and people. He has grown old amongst us, and our hope has been that the Lord would establish him in this parish. On this subject we made application to your Lordship some years ago, when we expressed what we thought of the valuable work going on here. God's truth has been faithfully and blessedly preached to many an anxious soul from the pulpit, from the press, in the cottage, and in the drawing-room. It has been taught to the lisping lips of childhood, and set forth as the map and guide of youth, the stay and comfort of age; that which was to be had "without money and without price." Doubtless He who allows not His word to return unto Him void, will bless those labours still further in His own good time, and will say unto His dear minister, "Well done, good and faithful servant, enter thou into the joy of thy Lord." Mr. —— has been blamed by many for the abrupt way in which he left. He was unable to do otherwise then; but has since returned, and we have been privileged once more to hear from that pulpit the voice we loved so long. Well did he take heed to Paul's exhortation, 1 Thess. v. 14. Oh, would that his stay had been prolonged, and his labours encouraged in our needy land. No less than nineteen Protestants and seven Roman Catholics, who were employed in his schools and otherwise, have been obliged to leave this parish to seek employment elsewhere. And now, thanking God, who first put it into your Lordship's heart to send him amongst us, we beg to sign ourselves,

Your Lordship's, &c.

For this address Alfred made the annexed acknowledgment:—

TO MY LATE PARISHIONERS AT BONMAHON.

Dearly beloved in the Lord,—Words would fail me if I were to attempt to express all I felt upon receipt of a copy of your letter addressed to my late Bishop; suffice it to say, it came in the most timely and opportune way. God be praised for it.

That you have, in any measure, been blessed and profited through the instrumentality of my humble labours, will be a matter of rejoicing to me during the remainder of my life, and, I doubt not, a source of wonder and adoring gratitude in eternity to come.

I thank God that I have been permitted once more to see and minister among you. After receiving your former affectionate address, it had been much laid upon my heart to make the attempt, as soon as the excitement of breaking up the schools, and the sale of my furniture, was over.

This desire, through God's mercy, has been granted; and, as you are aware, I was permitted also to visit my venerable rector, and to preach in his beautiful little church at Abbey, the last Sunday I spent in Ireland. The words selected for my text on the afternoon of that day—which occurred in the Psalms for the evening service—were certainly most congenial with my own feelings: "He that goeth forth and weepeth, bearing precious seed, shall doubtless come again with rejoicing, bringing his sheaves with him."

Both your former address to myself, and now that to my Bishop, has given me, dear people, the earnest of this blessed and happy "return." Yes, beloved, in the full sense of the word, the time will soon come. Be it ours to cherish the thought, and to rejoice in the prospect,—for

"Yet a season, and we know
Happy entrance shall be given;
All our sorrows left below,
And earth exchanged for heaven."

Our separation may well remind us of the words of the apostle James, "What is your life? It is even a vapour, that appeareth for a little time, and then vanisheth away." Think of how large a proportion of the ordinary life of men we have passed together. Within a few months of *one-fourth* of my life has been spent among you; and yet, in the review, what does it appear? Verily, like a dream. How true that word of the Psalmist, "We spend our years as a tale that is told;" and how very, very soon shall each of us "go the way of all flesh."

Oh that these things may increasingly be so laid upon our hearts, that our constant language may be, "So teach us to number our days, that we may apply our hearts unto wisdom."

Beloved, most earnestly do I desire that the Spirit may graciously act as the Remembrancer, in bringing to our minds much that we may have been enabled, by His grace and teaching, mutually to have considered. Bear in mind that the Holy Ghost is not confined to any times or seasons; and that He can, and does, "bring to remembrance" in the most vivid and profitable way, applying truths to the heart and mind with a freshness and savour that were even lacking when the self-same word was first spoken to the outward ear.

I cannot tell you how much you are upon my heart, nor can I express how frequently many of those seasons which we have mutually enjoyed in the house and service of the Lord, come to my recollection. These reflections would be attended with increased sorrow, but for the anticipation of that rapidly-approaching time when "the general assembly and Church of the first-born" shall meet around the throne, and where "God shall wipe away all tears from their eyes; and there shall be no more death, neither sorrow nor crying, neither shall there be any more pain; for the former things (shall have) passed away."

Before I close, there is one remark in your recent address to which I would advert—it is with reference to my apparently abrupt departure from among you. I say *apparently*, for you must remember how often I used to say, I felt sure my work was nearly done, and my time short among you. My enemies took advantage of this, and put an evil construction upon it. But, beloved, many of you knew, that, under existing circumstances, it was impossible for me to carry on the schools. As it was, I devoted nearly every shilling I possessed to the work of the Lord in Bonmahon. Had I remained longer, I should have been involved, and not, as now, have *settled every claim.* Moreover, the pressure upon my nerves, previous to my coming to the conclusion to which, soon after my arrival in England, I did come, was such, that (as I then told you) I was not equal to that formal leave-taking which the Lord afterwards strengthened me to undergo.

And now, in thanking you most sincerely for this renewed expression of attachment to myself, and appreciation of my humble labours among you, I cannot but acknowledge my deep sense of frailty and shortcoming in reference to the solemn trust so long reposed in me. Feeling my too great want of love and zeal and steadfastness in the great and important work of the ministry, I can but ask the Lord to pardon the sin of my most holy things, and take comfort from the fact, that His word declares He hath "hid the treasure in *earthen vessels*, that the excellency of the power may be of God, and not of us."

For yourselves, beloved, I pray that the Holy Ghost may reveal Jesus yet more and more, in and by the ministry of the word, and likewise in your own private meditation upon that word. Permit me to urge upon you anew the study of it. Seek to be alone at least some small portion of each day. Select the hour or half-hour when you are least likely to be intruded upon by domestic, social, or business claims. Let yours not be public nor family worship merely, but closet worship also. Retire to your own chamber; lock or bolt your door. Pray to your Father, and your Father which seeth in secret, Himself shall reward you openly. Oh, how sweet His "rewards." How precious those gifts received upon the knee of prayer. How blessed and how personal those answers which the Lord gives to the very petitions He Himself draws forth from the heart. These are among the means which bring a soul to the knowledge of the Lord, and to a precious realization of its interest in the Lord.

I cannot close without expressing my gratitude for one fact which has come to my knowledge—namely, that sundry of you meet every day, at a certain hour, at the throne of grace, purposely to ask a blessing for your late minister. I cannot tell you how this rejoices my heart. May the Lord hear your prayers on my behalf, and may your petitions be answered likewise abundantly to your own souls' comfort, refreshing, and establishment.

Seeing that as yet the Lord has not manifestively "fixed the bounds of my habitation," and placed me in another sphere of labour, Satan may take advantage of the same, and intimate that your prayers are not heeded. Beloved, let not this discourage you. Be mindful of the word I have often spoken to you, "We know but parts of His ways." We are called to walk by *faith*, and not by *sight*. Had I been debarred from *preaching*, through not being settled, my anguish of heart would be extreme. But so far from this being the case, many and many have been the open doors afforded me. It has been my exalted privilege, Sabbath after Sabbath, and once or twice on the evenings of each week, since I left you, to speak of and in that name which is above every name, and which is mutually dear to our hearts. Yes, to thousands upon thousands have I been permitted to minister; and not a few instances have come to my knowledge of the Lord blessing His word in a remarkable manner.

Dear, dear people, farewell. The Lord grant us to meet oftentimes in spirit at His footstool. (Yes, I do frequently meet you there.) And when we have done and suffered His will on earth, may we each and all meet around the throne, to cast our crowns at Immanuel's feet, and shout, "Victory, victory, through the blood of the Lamb."

I am, my dear friends,

Your affectionate pastor,

* * *

Plymouth, Aug. 21, 1858.

CHAPTER XLI.

DIFFICULTIES IN AN ENTERPRIZE OFTTIMES OVERRULED AS A STIMULUS—SATAN THE SURE OPPONENT OF EVERY GOOD WORK —THE OBJECT OF THIS BOOK TO ANIMATE AND ENCOURAGE OTHERS—THE NECESSITY FOR "TRYING AGAIN"—THE BENEFIT OF EXPERIENCE—APPOINTMENT OF ALFRED TO ANOTHER SPHERE OF LABOUR.

SOME considerable space has been occupied with the foregoing extracts, but it was necessary, for the sake of the connexion, and that the ultimate results and issue might the more clearly and encouragingly be seen. Moreover, it may prepare the mind of the reader for trial, and vexation, and disappointment, in relation to his earthly career, for it is next to impossible to pass through the present life without difficulties; and the more important the work in which men are led to engage, the more may they expect their character and conduct to be criticized. If the work be of God, Satan and the world will be sure to oppose. Hence the Apostle, on one occasion, said, "A great and effectual door is opened unto me, *and* (as though this were as a matter of course and of necessity) there are many adversaries."

The great object of this book has been to encourage the reader—the young especially—to seek wisdom and strength from above, in order that they might master the difficulties and overcome the obstacles which may —nay, which must—present themselves. We value but little that which costs us little. What has been achieved by dint of labour, or obtained by much perseverance, and long and continuous application, is the more highly esteemed and valued. Further, it calls into exercise one of the most desirable qualities—that of *patience*. What painter or poet, statesman or soldier, architect or artizan, ever accomplished anything without *patience?*

Again, when our hopes and expectations in one particular channel are cut off, it is not for us to sit down in despair, and say, "Well, I am defeated, and it is of no use for me any longer to TRY to get on." So far from this being a just conclusion, it is questionable whether the most successful men in the long run have not been men who have, perhaps, been subjected to defeat and disappointment. Where is the general who won *every* battle in which he ever engaged, or the admiral who *always* was victorious? And have not their very losses served, in the sequel, to lead the way to their greatest achievements? Is it not recorded of one of our most brilliant statesmen, that, upon his first appearance in the

House of Parliament, he stuttered and stammered, and was compelled abruptly to close his maiden speech? Vexed beyond measure within himself, he subsequently exclaimed, "It's *in me*, and it *shall* come out." He was resolved to TRY AGAIN. He did TRY AGAIN. He astounded the House with his eloquence, and speedily became one of, if not *the* first of the orators of his day. And where is the boy whose very failure has not prompted him to TRY AGAIN, and that, too, so successfully as to attain oftentimes to the highest position in the school, and thence, stimulated by that knowledge of the past, and experience of the present, prompted him, in other and still more important spheres, to his pursuing a course as grateful to himself as it has proved satisfactory to others?

Experience is a wonderful word, and experience is invariably based upon test and trial, and trial and test again. Experience presupposes diversity, and that diversity generally comprehends adversity as well as prosperity. That knowledge is of little worth which is not grounded upon test—upon personal observation and experience. The steersman shuns the quicksand, and the pilot the sunken reef upon which the ship was well-nigh wrecked. Lessons are every day, and all the day, put before us, and our aim and object should be so to learn those lessons as to turn them to account—to avoid the evil, and to choose the good. If we are observant, as it behoves us to be, we shall learn much by the career of others, as well as by our own mistaken steps and thoughtless enterprizes. Who, if he were going through life again, but would seek to avoid what has cost him many a heartache? Had he *seen* at first what he *proved* at last, how different his proceedings!

It has been said, that, when Alfred left Ireland, after so long a sojourn there, it seemed to be beginning life anew. He had sought to tarry—yea, to end his days—in the sister isle; but God had other and better things in store for him. There was one thing which had long weighed upon his spirit, and that was, *the very limited number committed to his charge.* Strictly speaking, he had but fifty Protestant parishioners, and these included children. The average attendance at church of some seventy or eighty souls was made up, in addition to his own people, of those who came from the borders of the adjoining parish. Hence, as far as preaching was concerned, it appeared at times to be a waste of energy, and he longed for the *many,* rather than the *few,* to whom to minister. The hope of converts from the Church of Rome was doomed to meet with disappointment, for the number was small indeed who, whatever their convictions of right and wrong, were prepared to combat the persecution that must necessarily follow the throwing off of Popery, and the open espousal of Protestantism. It was a case of this kind, indeed, that led to that series of bitter persecutions which Alfred had to encounter, and which led him, at length, to see his work in the locality where he had so long dwelt was nearly done, and to believe that God's providence was directing him to some other field of labour.

After-facts proved these suppositions to have been correct. He left Ireland; and, though some few months elapsed ere the place which God had designed for him was made known, yet in due time it was revealed; and it was revealed, too, in connexion with such a singular train of circumstances, as no observant eye could come to any other conclusion than that it was the finger of God which pointed out the parish and the people where and among whom he was to labour. That place was an offcut from a densely-populated parish, where, instead of sixty souls being allotted to him, upwards of six thousand were nominally committed to his care. Here a church had to be built, and schools established. Hence, after Alfred's unanimous appointment by gentlemen to whom (with one exception) he had previously been an utter stranger, it was deemed advisable, as a preliminary measure, to set up a temporary wooden building, so that divine service might be conducted in it, and form, for the time, a nursery for the permanent church. On the opposite page is a sketch of the temporary structure. Soon after it was opened, it was found necessary so to enlarge it as to accommodate little less than one thousand persons.

The facts just mentioned are briefly embodied in a speech made by one of the trustees, on his being called to the chair at what was termed a monster tea-meeting, which was given upon the occasion of the closing-up of the temporary church, the day after the consecration of the permanent building:—

The CHAIRMAN (John Drake, Esq.) said it was with a twofold feeling—of pleasure and regret—that he took the chair that evening, paradoxical as that statement might seem; but it was with regret that the duties had not devolved on a more competent person, and with pleasure that he was there that night to testify to the Incumbent the respect and regard in which he was held

by the worshippers accustomed to assemble there. From his intimate acquaintance with their beloved pastor, he could speak of him as a Christian minister and as a valued friend; but, as he was present, he (the Chairman) would forbear from doing so, lest it might be repugnant to the rev. gentleman's feelings. He (the speaker) looked on the present as a most interesting and solemn occasion, as they had met together for the last time in that humble building; and he rejoiced to think that many would bless the day on which that building was erected, for he looked on old associations —especially when they had been of a pleasant character—in the light of old friends, and parted from them with regret. He did think that a fitting occasion to praise the Almighty for His good and gracious dealings towards them, in permitting them so often to assemble in that humble building. He would, however, more particularly direct their attention to the new structure, and he thought they would bear with him while he did so. God's hand had been mercifully marked in all connected with the building, so that it plainly was *His* work. To Him, therefore, be all the praise and all the glory. (Applause.) About three years since, when he was a parishioner, and was walking in the grounds of his residence, there was a dear and valued friend of his, knowing the spiritual destitution of ——, asked him if he would give £500 towards the erection of the church, provided a suitable minister could be obtained; and he at once agreed to do so, though he saw but little prospect of the object proposed being accomplished. The same idea was afterwards communicated to three other members of his family, who cheerfully and willingly acquiesced in giving a like sum. That appeared to be a good beginning; but when he considered the amount of money required for a suitable structure, and for an endowment, his heart failed him. Within a short time after that, their excellent Bishop delivered an address at the Victoria Rooms, so replete with love and charity, that it could not fail to commend itself to all who loved Christ with sincerity and truth; and a large-hearted Dissenter of the city, the late Mr. Holmes, communicated to the trustees, through his representative, Mr. Inskip, that he would further their views by giving the munificent sum of £2,000, which was afterwards increased to £3,000. That he (the Chairman) considered to be a special mark of God's providence, for that came from a source apparently most unlikely. At that time the Incumbent was prosecuting a very successful work in Ireland, but from his fearless advocacy of the truth, he subjected himself to persecution, as was the case in many Roman Catholic countries; his life was threatened, and a Government reward had to be offered for the apprehension of the offender. That determined him at length to give up his post, not knowing where he was going. Now *that* he (the Chairman) considered another special mark of God's providence; for here was a man evidently set apart by God for a great work in —— although they knew it not. (Applause.) After that the panic of 1857 and 1858 occurred, and he thought they would agree with him that that was not a fitting time to solicit subscriptions for a new building, as every one was most intent on his own affairs; therefore the church remained for some time in abeyance; and at length a meeting of the trustees was held in Clifton, and Mr. Inskip attended, and informed them that Mr. Holmes required that they should immediately commence the building, and appoint the Rev. — —— incumbent, or else he (Mr. H.) would revoke his gift. Now he (the Chairman) must confess that he thought that that was very dictatorial, although he had since blessed God that Mr. Holmes had arrived at that determination. He (the Chairman) at once said, "And who is this Mr. ——?" and the trustees were then informed, that he had been carrying on a very successful work in Ireland, that he had given it up, and was then in England. The consequence was that a telegraphic message was despatched to him. The next day he appeared in B——, and, through the kindness of Mr. Clifford, preached the same evening at St. Matthew's. Many trustees attended, and so pleased were they with the sermon, that they felt convinced he was the right man. (Applause.) He thought the members of the congregation fully approved of that. (Applause.) Such, then, was the history of that church which, on Wednesday, was so solemnly and so beautifully devoted to the service of the Almighty. (Applause.) The Chairman then turned to the rev. gentleman, and spoke as follows:—And now, sir, it devolves on me—and it is the most pleasing part of my evening's duties—to present you with this salver, and with a purse of 100 sovereigns, or rather 102 sovereigns. I think I cannot do better than read the inscription on the salver:—

Presented to
The Rev. [— — ——],
with a purse of 100 sovereigns,
by his
congregation and friends,
as a testimonial of their high esteem
for his character and ministerial labours at the
Temporary Church,
during the erection of the
Church of St. [—— ——],
where they trust his future pastoral duties will be
crowned with the Divine blessing.
January 24, 1861.

I now present this testimonial, sir, in the name of the congregation and friends who have been in the habit of assembling here, in consideration of the ministerial duty you have performed in this place during the last twenty months; and I am sure it must be most gratifying to you, sir, to think that your labour of love, though of so short duration, has been so highly appreciated by them. I trust, sir, you will be spared many years to sow the good seed, and that with unsparing hand, not only in yonder building, but in the district generally; and, under the divine blessing, may it bring forth fruit abundantly, in some thirty, in some sixty, and in some a hundred fold. (Applause.)

The salver was of a massive description, weighing 37 oz., and of chaste workmanship; it was supplied by Mr. Taylor, of College Green. The 102 sovereigns were fresh from the Mint, and were enclosed in a most elegant purse. There were about 180 subscribers to this testimonial.

Of the church itself, and the consecration, the journals of the day thus speak:—

In the case of St. Luke's, we have reason to know that the Bishop of the diocese is no less pleased than surprised at the achievement which has been accomplished. A new church does not always mean religious progress; but St. Luke's is simply a church provided for a congregation which, two years ago, had no existence; and which, but for the marvellous exertions of the Incumbent, would never, according to ordinary calculation, have been gathered at all. The Incumbent has carried out the system which Dr. Chalmers describes as "excavating the heathen," and to-night, when his friends meet for the last time in the temporary wooden building, where his labours have been so prosperous, we expect to find them marking their sense of those labours in a manner alike substantial and pleasing.

Yesterday, the interesting and imposing ceremony of consecrating the Church of St. Luke, on the New Cut, was performed by the Right Rev. the Lord Bishop of

Gloucester and Bristol, in the presence of a congregation of nearly two thousand persons. His Lordship was attended by his Chancellor, C. J. Monk, Esq.; the Rural

Dean, the Rev. Humphrey Allen; and the Registrar, C. S. Clarke, Esq.; and everything passed off most successfully. The history, well-nigh romantic, of the stately and commodious structure, which rises just midway on the

road running between Bath Bridge and Bedminster Bridge, on the Bedminster side of the Cut, is so familiar to our readers, that we need only remind them, that it has risen within the short period of two years; that upwards of eleven thousand pounds have been subscribed towards its completion, by persons of all classes residing near and far from its immediate locality; that its spacious and noble interior will accommodate upwards of twelve hundred worshippers; and that at present all the requisite funds have been subscribed, with the exception of some few hundred pounds.

The endowment of the new church is £120 per annum, exclusive of certain seat rents. The majority of the seats are appropriated to the poor, free; and the remainder, which in no respect differ from the free seats, will be letable at a certain fixed sum per annum.

CHAPTER XLII.

THE NECESSITY FOR PAROCHIAL SCHOOLS—THEIR SATISFACTION TO THE MINISTER—SUNDAY SCHOOLS—PROPOSAL OF THE SCHOLARS TO BUILD—EXTRACTS FROM DIARY—ENCOURAGING PROPOSAL.

NO parish can be complete without schools; and, however large or interesting a congregation, it would speak but indifferently for the minister who could be satisfied to labour without seeking to make provision for the instruction of the rising generation. Nothing, in fact, can be more grateful to a parochial clergyman than to see the young of his flock placed under a regular course of teaching, on the week-days as well as on the Sundays, hoping that, with the blessing of Him who has said that "His word shall not return unto Him void, but that it shall accomplish that which He pleases, and that it shall prosper in the thing whereto He sent it," very many may grow up to be useful members of society; and, at last, both teachers and taught meet in that happy world where sin and sorrow are unknown.

We shall again let Alfred speak for himself. The simple statement of facts may serve the more to encourage others, and operate as a wholesome check should they be disposed "to despise the day of small things." Having felt the want of a school-building press heavily upon his heart, he one Sabbath afternoon spoke to the Sunday-school children upon the subject, as they were assembled in a room beyond the precincts of the parish. Having asked them what was to be done, the children, as with one voice, recommended that a school-house should be built; and, when again asked where the money was to come from for such a purpose, they with equal promptitude declared that *they* would give it. A little fellow immediately afterwards stepped up to the minister, and placed a *threepenny piece** in his hand. Seeing their heartiness in the matter, he at once went round the classes with a box, and some eight shillings in coppers were contributed. This induced Alfred, on behalf of the much-needed schools, to "TRY, AND TRY AGAIN." The task before him seemed a difficult one, considering the amount of money so recently collected, coupled with the fact that he was called to labour in so poor a parish. Moreover, a debt still remained on the

* This threepenny piece was afterwards deposited in the bottle which was set in the foundation-stone.

church, in consequence of its having been so very lately erected. Still there were Solomon's words prompting to action, "Whatsoever thy hand findeth to do, do it with thy might; for there is no work, nor device, nor knowledge, nor wisdom, in the grave, whither thou goest" (Eccl. ix. 10). Alfred's state of mind at this time is best expressed in his own words:—

Sunday, May 25th, 1862.—Oh, my God, what cause have I seen in myself to be deeply humbled before Thee, in reference to the work to which Thou hast been pleased to call me. In looking round this parish, and contemplating Thy hand and handiwork, during the last three years and a half, I am lost in wonder and amazement. I can only exclaim, "It is the Lord's doing, and it is marvellous in mine eyes." When I reflect upon the fact of the large amount that has been collected and expended in that period upon the church and endowment, I am almost astounded. Yet I blush withal to add, that, because there is a debt of some £650 still remaining upon the church, and a similar sum required for the schools now so greatly needed in this parish, yet I cannot look to the Lord, nor trust the Lord, as I would do, for the same. My carnal heart has, of late, been most wretchedly at work. Indifference, if not absolute unbelief, has had a deadly influence. I feel condemned—greatly so. I know full well, "I *have* not, because I *ask* not." Hence (though with trembling, for fear of the trial it may entail) I have been of late asking the Lord to lay the matter with *more weight* upon my heart. Strange as it may appear, I have been desiring *a greater burden* with regard to this church debt and these schools to be laid upon my shoulders, so that I may be compelled, more continuously and of more absolute necessity, to roll that self-same burden upon the Lord.

I may be wrong in this matter, and there may be more of the flesh in it than I am aware of, but my feeling is this, that *travail* must precede a *birth;* and I think I may say, that I have found a sweet and gracious deliverance has invariably followed the *wrestling* and *importunity*. I know it, by blessed experience, to be true, that "He who watches a Providence, shall never want a Providence to watch."

But I fear—and I confess it before my God—that I have of late been too much looking to *man*. I may truly say, that, if I do look to *man*, in place of looking to my *God*, I am sure to meet with disappointment and defeat. But if, on the contrary, I am inclined to go to my *God* first, to wrestle with *Him*—to importune *Him*—I see such blessed proofs afterwards that men's hearts are in the hands of God, and that He turns them like rivers of water in a dry place.

Moreover, I can testify, to the honour of my God, that I find it *easier*, as well as infinitely more *blessed*, to ask anything of my *God* than *man*. I make but a very poor hand of it, if I go to solicit anything of the *creature;* but, if I go to ask anything of my *God*, I go under the full consciousness that He, my Father, knoweth what I have need of.

Lord, do Thou, therefore, so pour out upon me a spirit of grace and supplication, and so give me to watch and acknowledge Thy hand in the matter of this church-debt and these schools, that this very book may bear testimony that Thou art still the God who heareth and answereth prayer.

Wednesday morning, May 28th.—I come this morning

to record before the Lord renewed proofs of His most tender, merciful, and gracious dealings. Since Sunday, I have been filled with adoring wonder at the Lord's condescension and mercy. Verily He has afresh proved Himself to be the God who hears and answers prayer. I sat here in the interval of worship on Sunday, under a deep sense of *all* hearts being in the Lord's hands, and of *His* being able to move those hearts without any *human* help or interference; and in this spirit I wanted simply to look to and lean upon the Lord, and the Lord alone.

My subject on Sunday was, "Your heavenly Father knoweth that ye have need of all these things." When speaking of the want of faith, I remarked, in the most unpremeditated way, how painfully I felt rebuked on the Friday previously, when a friend took me for a couple of hours' drive round by Mr. Müller's Orphan Asylum Houses. When I recollected that little, if anything, short of £75 *a-day* was wanted to meet the necessities of that establishment, I felt ashamed of myself before the Lord, that I could not trust Him for the trivial sum still wanted in this parish. I could but chide myself for my unbelief, and felt I could cover my face with my hands, and prostrate myself in the very dust before God. "Out of the abundance of the heart the mouth spoke."

On Monday morning, deeply imbued with the subject, I went over to Bath, to consult an architect, a dear friend and brother in the Lord, in regard to the schools. I told him my want of a simple, plain, commodious building; and that as yet I had but about £400 in money and promises towards both land and structure. He directly most generously said he would give a donation towards the work.

I should have said, that at our Monday-morning prayer-meeting, which I attended prior to going to Bath, I requested the brethren present to lay the matter of the schools specially before the Lord. Three prayed; and, if I may speak for the rest, we found the presence of the Lord. He was in our midst, and the season was a sacred one, though our number did not exceed a dozen persons.

On the evening of that day, one of the congregation (to my perfect astonishment) told me that the matter of the schools had been very much laid upon his mind. It was the friend to whom I just now alluded as having driven me on Friday round by the Orphan Asylum. When we left home it was quite with another view; but the gentleman whom we went purposely to see being from home, my friend said, "Where shall we drive? Have you seen the new Orphan Asylum?" This led to our going thither, and to the Lord's subsequent working by that simple circumstance.

From this friend's conversation, therefore, on the Monday evening, I gathered that on Sunday afternoon, *at the very time I was recording before the Lord the fact that all hearts were in His hand*, and that He could turn them as seemed good in His sight, he had said to his wife, that he thought he would add a codicil to his will, leaving £100 to the schools. "Why wait for your *death?*" was her answer. "Give it *now*, in your lifetime."

[Oh, what responsibility devolves upon wives! What a mighty influence do *they* exercise over their husbands! It is the wives that in this sense build the churches, and the chapels, and the school-houses. A much greater responsibility devolves upon them than they are wont to imagine. It was a wife who, under God, first started the idea that led to all that has been done in this parish during the last three years and a half.]

The issue of that conversation was the following plain, matter-of-fact letter, under date

May 27, 1862.

Dear Sir,—We (that is, the writer and his wife) have been consulting in reference to the proposed schools, and, thinking that they are quite as essential in the parish as the church, we feel sorry more has not been done. We have, therefore, come to the conclusion, that the Lord having been so good to us, we should do something in return; and propose, if you can find any party that will give one-half the ground, I will give the other. I think, with Mrs. D——, that a sum given to set the work going, may be more real value than double the sum given by *will*, besides saving the expenses attending such legacy.

My impression is, if you could secure the land, and make a fair start, funds would be forthcoming as the work advances, and that we should see the building free of debt within a short time of its completion. I make this proposal from the conviction that the schools are so much needed; not that the parish has any claim on me in a business point of view.

We should consider that the summer is now fast passing away, and, if anything for the schools is done, they should be commenced forthwith.

Remaining, my dear Sir, faithfully yours,

G. D——.

Words fail to express what I felt upon my knowledge of the aforementioned conversation, and upon receipt of this letter. I could only fall before the Lord in adoring wonder and admiration. Last evening I took it and laid it before one who has already been a large and one of the foremost contributors to the work. After a little conversation, he most kindly and generously consented to contribute the other half of the ground. "Bless the Lord, O my soul, and all that is within me bless His holy name."

Saturday night, May 31.—The close of this week and month calls indeed for thanksgiving and praise to the Lord for His boundless mercy and goodness in that which has been pressing upon my heart. To the promise of the aforementioned contribution of the ground for the schools, which has this week been purchased for £250, I have to add for this day's receipts a further sum of £23 13s. 10d., making for the week no less a sum than £273 13s. 10d.!

Wednesday morning, June 10, 1862.—Once again, O Lord, would I appeal to Thee on behalf of these schools. I have, as it were, committed myself to Thee and them. I have publicly declared, that, notwithstanding the amount still wanted, I believed that we should occupy those schools before Christmas, whereas as yet not a stone is laid towards their erection. Lord, I have ventured upon Thyself. It is, I trust, a simple matter of faith. If it is *faith*, as I hope it is, put it not to confusion, but, agreeably to Thy word, may it be seen, "According to thy faith, be it unto thee." Now here, Lord, would I take my stand. Here would I plead. From Thee would I not waver, but simply cleave to Thee and to Thy word. Make bare Thine arm, I beseech Thee. Go forth in delivering acts. Let me see Thy wondrous doings, and have fresh grounds to testify of the same.

June 13.—Received yesterday £1 10s., and this day £10, for the schools. The Lord be praised for His many and great mercies. This evening, the Lord permitting, the Building Committee meet for the purpose of receiving tenders for the erection of the building. May the Lord manifestively be present, and direct our minds in the selection. May all move on clearly under His sweet smile and approving will. Step by step may we see and acknowledge the Lord's hand, giving Him the glory due to His adorable name.

Evening.—Since writing the foregoing, £30 more has been added to our fund; and this evening, out of thirty-three tenders, one has been accepted, amounting to £1,035. The sum seems large, but it is nothing with our God. Lord, give more faith, that we may look to Thee, wrestle with Thee, wait for and expect a blessing at Thy hand. Keep me from conferring with flesh and blood. Enable me simply and ardently to cleave to Thyself; and, oh, in spite of all fleshly feeling and fear, open, I pray Thee, Thy heart and Thy hand.

Saturday morning, June 14th.—Exercised about the proceedings of the last evening; but I desire, O Lord, to be enabled to roll my burden upon Thyself, the Burden-bearer. I have found the blessedness of so doing times without number. Oh, grant me grace from Thyself, in this new care and anxiety, to "commit my way unto the Lord, to trust also in Him, that *He* may bring it to pass." Lead me, Lord, in a very special and gracious manner to learn the sweetness and power that is involved in that one word, *trust*. I would "walk by faith, not by sight." I delight to tell Thee that all hearts are in Thy hands, and that the "cattle upon a thousand hills are Thine," as well as the gold and the silver. My faith may be sorely tried in the matter of these schools, but "Thou wilt work, and who shall let or hinder?" Oh, give me more grace, so that I may wait earnestly and ardently upon Thee, and watch most closely Thy kind and gracious doings. "Is anything too hard for the Lord?" No, Lord, no; blessed be Thy great and glorious name! Though *I* may not know *how* or *where*, this book, I feel assured, shall testify of what Thy power—what Thy love—what Thy condescending and merciful answers to the breathings of poor sinners. Thou art now, as of old, the God who heareth and answereth prayer. Only give me a single eye to Thyself!

Monday morning, June 16.—Yesterday was the fifteenth anniversary of my ordination; and, as I sat in the evening listening to my dear son, as he preached for the first time in our new church of St. Luke's, I said within myself, "What hath God wrought!" and greatly indeed did I feel the power of the hymn which he himself had selected, in which this verse occurs:—

"He who hath helped us hitherto,
Will help us all our journey through;
And daily give us cause to raise
New Ebenezers to His praise."

At the close of the service, which was attended by a large congregation, the subjoined letter was handed to me by the sexton:—

Dear Sir,—Will you have the kindness to desire your publisher to forward me six copies of your new book as soon as published? I enclose the money for them, which I believe is £1 4s.; also, a donation of £25 towards the funds for the new schools.

I am leaving home for some weeks to-morrow morning, and remain,

Dear Sir, yours, very truly,

* * *

Thus did the Lord crown yesterday—a very special day in my experience—with His most gracious favour; and thus did He encourage me to give heed to the text of the morning, "Commit thy way unto the Lord, trust also in Him, and *He* shall bring it to pass."

[Subsequently to the receipt of the note just quoted, I have received two cheques, the one for £10 10s., the other for £10. I have signed the contract for the building of the schools for the sum of £1,035; the foundation-stone of which the Mayor of Bristol has consented to lay on the 3rd of July.

"Triumphant faith the promise sees,
And trusts to Christ alone;
Laughs at impossibilities,
And cries, It *shall* be done."]

CHAPTER XLIII.

COMMENCEMENT OF SCHOOL-BUILDING—LAYING THE FOUNDATION-STONE BY THE MAYOR AND MAYORESS OF BRISTOL—LARGE TEA-MEETINGS—AGED PARISHIONERS—DEATH OF ALFRED'S DAUGHTER—CONCLUSION.

IN accordance with the hope expressed at the close of the last chapter, the Mayor of Bristol, accompanied by the Mayoress, attended in state upon the given date, for the purpose of laying the foundation-stone of the proposed schools. After a slight shower or two in the forenoon, the day cleared up, and became all that could be desired. The attendance was very large, and the whole scene of the most interesting description. The journals of the day thus recorded the event:—

The foundation-stone of schools proposed to be erected in connexion with St. Luke's Church, was laid on the

3rd ult., by the Right Worshipful the Mayor, John Hare, Esq. The want of commodious schools in the large and rapidly-extending district in which St. Luke's Church is situated, and which is inhabited for the most part by persons of the humbler classes, has long been felt; and the respected incumbent, considering that the present mode of conducting the schools, namely, in sundry hired rooms, was in a measure unsatisfactory and objectionable, determined upon making an effort to raise a fund for the erection of a plain and substantial school building, and, from the liberal response which has already been made to the rev. gentleman's appeal, and with a lively recollection of past success in a much greater undertaking, we have no doubt that the sum now remaining unsubscribed will speedily be raised, and that the schools may be opened free from the incumbrance of debt.

The site of the proposed school is about three hundred yards from St. Luke's Church. The style of the building will be plain Early English, and, as the trustees have wisely determined to raise it as economically as possible, there will be no attempt at ornamentation. The building will comprise one large schoolroom, 94 ft. by 36 ft., two class-rooms, offices, and other conveniences, with two capacious playgrounds in front. The estimated cost of the erection is £1,035, and the school is intended to accommodate 600 children.

A hymn having been sung, the Rev. Canon Madan, vicar of St. Mary Redcliff, offered up an appropriate prayer. A handsome silver trowel was presented to his Worship by the churchwardens, which bore the following inscription:—"Presented to the Worshipful the Mayor of Bristol, John Hare, Esq., upon the occasion of his laying the foundation-stone of the Parochial Schools of

St. Luke's, Bedminster, on the 3rd July, 1862. John Drake, Esq., George Duck, Esq., churchwardens." His Worship spread the mortar in true masonic style, and the stone being lowered into its position, he struck it with the mallet, and tested its level with the square, after which he repeated the following prayer:—"Forasmuch as Almighty God once accepted the purpose of Solomon to build a house unto His name, and nothing doubting but that He favourably alloweth this work of ours, to found and erect this building for His service, we therefore lay this chief corner-stone in the name of the great Jehovah, the holy, holy, holy, undivided Trinity, Father, Son, and Holy Ghost, three Persons, but one God, blessed for evermore. Amen."

The Mayoress deposited, in a cavity made in the stone, a bottle containing the following inscription:—"To the Triune Jehovah, this, the chief corner-stone of the schools for the parish of St. Luke's, Bedminster, in the city and county of Bristol, was laid on the 3rd day of July, 1862, in the 26th year of the reign of Her Majesty Queen Victoria, by the Right Worshipful the Mayor."

His Worship then addressed the large company who had assembled to witness the ceremony. He said—When a short time since, their incumbent did him the honour to request him to take so prominent a part in that interesting ceremony, he acceded to his request with great pleasure; for he conceived that his time, energies, and influence could not be better bestowed than in laying the foundation-stone of those schools, which, under God's blessing, he trusted would prove the foundation of good to all classes of the community. It was impossible for them to ignore the fact, that, if they wished to ameliorate the condition of the poorer classes, it must be done by means of education. There was no doubt that much had already been done, but it was also equally certain that a great deal more was required to be done. Almsgiving was all very well in its way—he was not referring to that indiscriminate kind of almsgiving to sturdy beggars and such like; he referred to almsgiving in those cases which they well knew to be genuine. If they educated their poor, however, they superseded, to a great extent, the necessity of almsgiving. His Worship went on to remark upon the great value of education, and said that many and many a man literally and truly stood the chance of being starved because he was altogether deficient of education. An utterly uneducated man was a very dependent being, and was altogether helpless, while a person with a certain amount of education was enabled to weather the storm, which, under other circumstances, he would not be enabled to do. Only a few days since, last Sunday week, he had attended the gaol, and had been deeply impressed with the sight. He could not help thinking of the words of an early reformer, John Bradford, who said, when he saw a poor criminal being led to execution, "But for the grace of God, there goes John Bradford." That great and good man subsequently suffered at the stake, and he had no doubt that in his hour of trial he was supported by his faith, and that he realized the words of the poet—

> "Behind a frowning Providence,
> He hides a smiling face;"

and therefore, when he looked at those poor creatures, bound in dens, lost outcasts of society, he could not help feeling that but for the grace of God, *he* might have been among that miserable crew. What made the scene more impressive was the service of the day—on that day they had the solemn parable of Dives and Lazarus. He felt, as it were, that those solemn words were addressed to him, and that if he neglected to do his duty in his station of life according to the best of his ability, there would be a heavy reckoning for him hereafter. What referred to him referred to all; and in no possible way could they be more profitably engaged in God's service than in endeavouring, according to the best of their means, to relieve the distress and wants of their poorer fellow-citizens. His Worship said, that, according to the last census, the population of that district, of which their incumbent had charge, was 6,434 souls. The churchwardens had generously presented the land for the schools, which they had purchased for £250, being a sum far less than it was worth, in consideration of its being for schools. Already a sum of £600 and upwards had been promised towards their erection.

Various portions of Scripture were read by the clergy present, a hymn sung, prayer offered, and the proceedings terminated with the Rev. S. A. Walker pronouncing the benediction.

A few months later, and the public journals spoke of the work again as follows :—

The completion of these schools was celebrated by a monster tea meeting. The tables were laid in the large room, the dimensions of which are probably not surpassed in any similar building in this city, and upwards of 900 persons were present. Much satisfaction was expressed not only at the manner in which the arrangements were carried out, but also with the convenient character of the school buildings, which have been erected in an incredibly short space of time, under the auspices of the incumbent of St. Luke's. The gratification, however, of those present was somewhat alloyed in consequence of the serious illness of the daughter of

ST. LUKE'S SCHOOLS, BEDMINSTER.

the rev. gentleman, which prevented his taking any active part in the proceedings, and great sympathy was felt for him. After the tea a public meeting was held, and accommodation was found for some 600 more people, but notwithstanding there were still numbers who were anxious to gain admission, and the doors had eventually to be closed in order to avoid any accident from overcrowding.

The following evening a tea meeting was given to the aged parishioners of St. Luke's, Bedminster, by the respected incumbent. All the old people in the district over sixty years had been invited, and there was one patriarch present who was nearly one hundred years of age. For such of the old people as could not walk with comfort, a vehicle was hired of Mr. Payne, of Temple Gate. The Chairman announced the respective ages of those who composed the company present. There were nineteen aged 60, twenty-two aged 61, sixteen aged 62, fifteen aged 63, eleven aged 64, fourteen aged 65, seven aged 66, five aged 67, nine aged 68, six aged 69, twelve aged 70, three aged 71, five aged 72, five aged 73, six aged 74, six aged 75, three aged 76, five aged 77, two aged 78, two aged 79, one aged 80, three aged 81, two aged 82, two aged 83, one aged 84, two aged 90, and one aged 98. The Chairman said, that, whilst reading those numbers, he was struck by the thought of what a mercy it would be if they should all be together hereafter in that happy world where there would not be, as now, death in prospect, but where, having passed all sorrow, there would be no more tears to flow, no sighs, no groans to heave. Later in the evening the rev. gentleman said that there were 185 persons present, whose united ages amounted to 12,470 years, and the average age of each was 67½ years. The proceedings were diversified by some hymns which were sung at intervals, and at one part of the evening an old man, upwards of 80 years of age, and who had been blind for more than sixty years, offered up a fervent prayer. Altogether the meeting was of the most interesting character.

Just as the benediction was being pronounced, the Chairman's daughter, before referred to, died!

Hence the accomplishment of what had laid so near his heart—namely, the erection of his parochial schools—stands lastingly identified with one of the keenest sorrows of his little eventful life—the removal by death of a precious child of fifteen years of age, who had herself taken the deepest interest in the progress of the building, and whose last out-door engagement was the selection and purchase of some little reward books for her Sunday-class.

It is time, however, that the attention of the reader was relieved. It has been taxed far beyond the writer's intention. The reader will, it is hoped, take encouragement from the foregoing simple and uncoloured narrative to TRY, and, should difficulties present themselves, not be discouraged, but TRY AGAIN.

It now only remains for the author to thank his readers for the patient perusal they have afforded his unpretending volume; and to acknowledge with thankfulness that wise and mysterious Providence which, from very infancy, has watched over, guided, preserved, and provided for DAVID ALFRED DOUDNEY, the humble Incumbent of St. Luke's, Bedminster.

APPENDIX.

AS this little volume will doubtless fall into the hands of some who, sooner or later, may be engaged in works of a similar nature, it is more than probable that such would be pleased with additional particulars in regard to the funds with which the Church and Schools were erected. The following, therefore, is a simple analysis of the amount collected for the Church and endowment:—

	£	s.	d.
An anonymous donor	3,000	0	0
From Trustees, Richard and John Drake, Esqs., and John and William Cox, Esqs., £500 each	2,000	0	0
Incorporated Society	500	0	0
Sir Greville Smith, Bart.	250	0	0
W. H. G. Langton, Esq., M.P.	150	0	0
Diocesan Society	100	0	0
Anonymous	100	0	0
The late J. P., Esq., and George Jenkins, Esq., £50 each	100	0	0
Miss R., £25, £25, £10, £3	63	0	0
C. Finzel, Esq., £20, £25, £10	55	0	0
J. Boobyer, Esq., £25, £25, £25..	75	0	0
Sir W. Miles, Bart., M.P.	30	0	0

	£	s.	d.
Seven subscribers of £25 each	175	0	0
Eleven subscribers of £20 each	220	0	0
One subscriber of £15, one of £10 10s., and fifty-one of £10 each	535	10	0
Two gentlemen, towards coloured windows ..	32	0	0
Anonymous £7, M. F. £6, pupils of Misses Wright's school, £6 6s.	19	6	0
Nine subscribers at £5 5s. each	47	5	0
One hundred and fourteen subscribers at £5 each	570	0	0
Two subscribers at £4 4s. and £4..	8	4	0
Five subscribers at £3 3s.	15	15	0
Thirteen subscribers at £3..	39	0	0
Five subscribers at £2 10s.	12	10	0
Twenty-four subscriptions at £2 2s.	50	8	0
Sixty-five subscriptions at £2	130	0	0
One £1 15s., two £1 11s., four £1 10s., one £1 6s., one £1 5s. 6d.	13	8	6
Two £1 5s., one £1 4s. 6d., one £1 3s., one £1 2s. 6d., forty-four £1 1s.	52	4	0
Two hundred and thirteen £1, one hundred and twenty 10s.	273	0	0
One 16s., four 15s., one 14s., one 13s., one 12s. 6d., two 12s., one 9s., one 8s., six 7s. 6d., two 6s. 6d.	11	10	6
Three 10s. 6d.	1	11	6
Eight 6s., one 5s. 6d., eighty-one 5s., one 4s. 8d., two 4s. 6d., seven 4s., six 3s. 6d., eighteen 3s.	29	0	6
Twenty-three 2s. 6d., three 2s., three 1s. 6d., three 1s., one 4d., one 1d.	3	11	4
Cards	895	9	10
Ditto	14	12	8
Collections	483	11	6
Postage stamps	123	0	1
Boxes	9	7	0
Interest	29	15	3
Per *Gospel Magazine*	85	9	0

If asked how or in what proportions the various sums came in, the best reply may be gathered from the annexed simple record, as a specimen, quoted from "Memoranda of Church and School Matters," under date January, 1860:—

	£	s.	d.
Jan. 5th. Received this day..........	12	3	6
„ 6th	4	2	6
„ 7th	3	3	7
„ 8th—9th	11	13	0
„ 10th	10	3	0
[The 3s. was from a servant, who writes that she has been a subscriber to the *Gospel Magazine* ever since my editorship, twenty years in May next.]			
Jan. 11th	6	6	8
„ 12th	1	10	6
„ 13th	8	4	6
„ 14th	7	4	7
[For this week, £45 2s. 3d.]			
Jan. 15th—16th	5	15	2
„ 17th	3	9	6
„ 18th	1	7	6
„ 19th	85	0	2
„ 20th	9	3	11
„ 21st	7	16	6
[This week, £112 12s. 9d. ! !]			
Jan. 22nd—23rd	8	19	1
„ 24th	1	18	0
„ 25th	1	13	6
„ 26th	19	11	0
„ 27th	27	3	4
„ 28th	7	19	4
[This week, £67 4s. 3d.]			
For the four weeks, £324 9s.			
Jan. 29th—30th	1	1	6
„ 31st	3	2	0
Feb. 1st..........	5	14	0

	£	s.	d.
Feb. 2nd	2	7	10
„ 3rd	2	10	6
„ 4th	18	7	4
[For the week, £33 3s. 4d.]			
Feb. 5th—6th	5	12	7
„ 7th	2	15	7
„ 8th	19	7	6
„ 9th	0	8	0
„ 10th	0	15	0
„ 11th	2	10	2
[This week, £31 8s. 10d.]			
Feb. 12th—13th	6	7	3
„ 14th	5	12	6
„ 15th	1	6	0
„ 16th	0	7	11
„ 17th	6	5	6
„ 18th	0	2	6
[The week, £20 1s. 8d.]			
Feb. 19th—20th	1	1	5
„ 21st	15	0	9
„ 22nd	0	2	0
„ 23rd	6	3	0
„ 24th	14	11	8
„ 25th	9	0	7
[For the week, £45 19s. 5d.]			
For the month, £130 13s. 3d.			
Feb. 26th—27th	2	15	6
„ 28th	1	0	7
„ 29th	0	7	6
Mar. 1st	1	3	7
„ 2nd	1	16	0
„ 3rd	10	14	5
[The week, £17 17s. 1d.]			

	£	s.	d.
Mar. 4th—5th	0	6	0
„ 6th	1	2	6
„ 7th	13	8	0
„ 8th	2	3	8
„ 9th	3	0	6
„ 10th	0	2	0
[The week, £20 2s. 8d.]			
Mar. 11th—12th	0	2	6
„ 13th	0	8	6
„ 14th	2	0	0
„ 15th	1	10	0

	£	s.	d.
Mar. 16th	11	6	0
„ 17th	0	10	0
[The week, £15 16s.]			
Mar. 18th—19th	1	2	0
„ 20th	6	9	1
„ 21st	19	3	8
„ 22nd	0	15	9
„ 23rd	2	6	5
„ 24th	0	15	1
[The week, £30 12s.]			
For that month, £84 7s. 9d.			
For the twelve weeks, £539 1s.			

In looking over the Subscription-list, some facts recur to the memory, which may be interesting to the reader.

The first and largest item, which will at once arrest the eye, was that contributed by a retired Bristol merchant, who rose from the greatest obscurity to be so wealthy as to give away upwards of £80,000 during his lifetime. He never married, lived in the utmost retirement, and, though he took so kind an interest in the appointment of the writer to the parish of St. Luke's, he was never admitted to an interview with him; consequently they were not personally known to each other. It is said, that during his life, Mr. H—— (the merchant in question) had applications from various quarters for more than a million and a half of money. Upon this principle, one can understand why some persons contribute anonymously.

In singular contrast with the above, there stands a contributor —this individual was also personally unknown to the writer—who, from similar obscurity to the forementioned, had so risen as to accumulate immense wealth, little short, it is believed, of a quarter of a million of money. But, alas! instead of dispensing it, as did his fellow-townsman, for the benefit of society at large, he hoarded it with tenacious hand to the very verge of the grave. At length, from old age and infirmity, he was compelled to relinquish his grasp. The contribution—a comparatively small one—which, after much appeal, he made to the object in question, was regarded by those who knew him as an almost-astounding fact. Such a history is suggestive of much painful reflection, and may well beget a wholesome caution in those who, as the Apostle says, "will be rich," and who forget that "we brought nothing into this world, and it is certain we can carry nothing out." "Be not thou afraid," says the Psalmist, "when one is made rich, when the glory of his house is increased; for, when he dieth, he shall carry nothing away; his glory shall not descend after him."

An item of £25 stands early on the list. This was the offering of a beloved Christian brother, who, shortly after, sent another and another like amount, altogether unsolicited.

Another £25 stands on the list; this also was quickly succeeded by another of a similar amount. When in the neighbourhood of the donor's residence, some time afterwards, the writer sought personally to thank her. Instead of finding her, as he had previously supposed, occupying a mansion, her little house and whole appearance was of the most simple and unpretending character. Her object was to deny herself—to live in the simplest and most primitive way—and to devote her substance to the Lord. She has been altogether a contributor of £63 to St. Luke's Church; and has given largely also to other causes.

One item of £20 stands on the list, the free-will offering of a London baker, altogether unsolicited as far as the writer is concerned.

Another £20 presents itself on the list. This was contributed by an unknown lady, as a thank-offering for mercies received.

Another voluntary offering of £25, reminds the writer that the giver is now with a large family on the wide-spread ocean, bound for a far-distant land. May the God of Jacob watch over him and his!

£10. This reminds the writer of his first interview with the giver. "I hope you will pardon me," said he to the merchant in question, "for calling upon you without an introduction. "You did not need it," was the answer. The object was then placed before him; and the munificence of the gifts with which the list was opened. The fact that one had given £80,000 during his life, happened to be mentioned in the conversation. "I don't wish to boast," was the reply, "but *I* have given more than that. I have given away upwards of £90,000;" and, taking from his drawer a little penny memorandum-book, after a moment's glance at it, he remarked, "I see it is more than £9,000 this year already, and the year is young yet." It was the month of February. "Well," said the writer, "I hope you have found the truth of the Scripture, 'It is ——'" interrupting him, and taking the words from his lips, the merchant continued, "'more blessed to give than to receive.' Yes," he added, "and I am determined not to save." That merchant rose likewise from obscurity, and not merely made, but dispensed in his life-time, a princely fortune. In a few months after the interview in question, he was suddenly called to his rest; "and his works do follow him." Oh, what multitudes there are who deny themselves the greatest luxury in the world—*the luxury of giving.* And, in their anxiety to become rich, they altogether lose sight of the scriptural declaration—read in their ears, too, at some of the most solemn of life's fleet moments, the committing of friends and relatives to the silent grave—"Behold, Thou hast made my days as an handbreadth; and mine age is as nothing before Thee: verily every man at his best state is altogether vanity. Selah. Surely every man walketh in a vain show: surely they are disquieted in vain: *he heapeth up riches, and knoweth not who shall gather them*" (Ps. xxxix. 5, 6). The pride of the human heart is, upon the part of some men, carried to so fearful an extreme, that they actually wish it to be said, when they die, how rich they died! How awful a sin is this! How do such men overlook the fact, that at the last great day they will be called to account for their abused and mis-spent talents. "When the Son of man shall come in His glory, and all the holy angels with Him, then shall He sit upon the throne of His glory: and before Him shall be gathered all nations: and He shall separate them one from another, as a shepherd divideth his sheep from the goats: and He shall set the sheep on His right hand, but the goats on the left. Then shall the King say unto them on His right hand, Come, ye blessed of my Father, inherit the kingdom prepared for you from the foundation of the world: for I was an hungred, and ye gave me meat: I was thirsty, and ye gave me drink: I was a stranger, and ye took me in: naked, and ye clothed me: I was sick, and ye visited me: I was in prison, and ye came unto me. Then shall the righteous answer Him, saying, Lord, when saw we Thee an hungred, and fed Thee? or thirsty, and gave Thee drink? When saw we Thee a stranger, and took Thee in? or naked, and clothed Thee? Or when saw we Thee sick, or in prison, and came unto Thee? And the King shall answer and say unto them, Verily I say unto you, Inasmuch as ye have done it unto one of the least of these my brethren, ye have done it unto me. Then shall He say also unto them on the left hand, Depart from me, ye cursed, into everlasting fire, prepared for the devil and his angels: for I was an hungred, and ye gave me no meat: I was thirsty, and ye gave me no drink: I was a stranger, and ye took me not in: naked, and ye clothed me not: sick, and in prison, and ye visited me not. Then shall they also answer Him, saying, Lord, when saw we Thee an hungred, or athirst, or a stranger, or naked, or sick, or in prison, and did not minister unto Thee? Then shall He answer them, saying, Verily I say unto you, Inasmuch as ye did it not to one of the least of these, ye did it not to me. And these shall go away into everlasting punishment: but the righteous into life eternal" (Matt. xxv. 31—46). "There was a certain rich man, which was clothed in purple and fine linen, and fared sumptuously every day: and there was a certain beggar named Lazarus, which was laid at his gate, full of sores, and desiring to be fed with the crumbs which fell from the rich man's table: moreover, the dogs came and licked his sores. And it came to pass, that the beggar died, and was carried by the angels into Abraham's bosom: the rich man also died, and was buried; and in hell he lift up his eyes, being in torments, and seeth Abraham afar off, and Lazarus in his bosom. And he cried and said, Father Abraham, have mercy on me, and send Lazarus, that he may dip the tip of his finger in water, and cool my tongue, for I am tormented in this flame. But Abraham said, Son, remember that thou in thy lifetime receivedst thy good things, and likewise Lazarus evil things: but now he is comforted, and thou art tormented. And beside all this, between us and you there is a great gulf fixed: so that they which would pass from hence to you cannot; neither can they pass to us, that would come from thence. Then he said, I pray thee therefore, father, that thou wouldst send him to my father's house: for I have five brethren; that he may testify unto them, lest they also come into this place of torment. Abraham saith unto him, They have Moses and the prophets; let them hear them. And he said, Nay, father Abraham: but if one went unto them from the dead, they will repent. And he said unto him, If they hear not Moses and the prophets, neither will they be persuaded, though one rose from the dead" (Luke xvi. 19—31).

Riches involve upon the temporary possessor the most terrible of responsibilities; and, when a man wishes to be rich, he little knows how perilous a position he desires to occupy.

Another £10. As the giver walked round his very beautiful grounds, in the suburbs of London, he spoke both of the unsatisfactory as well as uncertain nature of riches, and intimated that he was a happier man before he retired from business. Here was one among the many examples which are daily presenting themselves, that reasonable and at least moderate occupation is so good for mankind in general.

Another £10. The giver, a perfect stranger previously. As there is not the least probability whatever of recognition in these comments, the writer may state with what pleasure he heard, from good authority, of the course adopted by this gentleman in regard to his gifts. In him (according to the testimony of a neighbouring parochial clergyman) is a striking illustration of Matt. vi. 3, "Let not thy left hand know what thy right hand doeth."

Another £10 from a somewhat distant town, given in memory of a late father, personally known to the writer.

Another £10, contributed by the readers of the *Gospel Magazine* in New York.

£5 from Plymouth, contributed in remembrance of a deceased

husband, much beloved by the writer. This was followed by a sum of £5 from the same source.

£5 from the aged widow of a deceased clergyman, well known for his contributions to the literature of the day.

£5, the voluntary offering of the widow of a deceased doctor, soon after called to her rest.

£5 5s. Gal. vi. 10.

£6 12s. 6d. "A little help by a little helper."

£5 from a clergyman, in acknowledgment of a letter of sympathy, under circumstances of most sudden and painful bereavement.

£5 from one who, a few weeks afterwards, was most suddenly called to his account. In one short week his wife was a bride and a widow. "In the midst of life we are in death."

£5. "A thank-offering for mercies received during, and recovery from, a long illness."

£5. To the memory of a departed sister.

£10. "A small thank-offering from Rochdale."

£5. "A Lover of the Truth," Baltimore.

£7. Left by "Anomymous" at the house.

£1. A thank-offering by one of the congregation.

£3 4s. 6d. collected by "A Worker for *Old Jonathan*."

4d. A little girl.

£20 and £25, from one who seeks to tread in his father's footsteps; that father has previously been referred to.

£20 from "Lovers of the Truth" (Ps. ciii. 11 and 14; Ps. cxvi. 12).

£25 from a blind gentleman in Lancashire.

£370 2s. 8¾d. Cards 1 to 288. The day upon which the proceeds of these cards were brought in to the vestry of the temporary church, was one of the most gratifying of the writer's life. The day itself was exceedingly wet, but the interest manifested by those who had taken cards was most delightful. One plain, unpretending person said, her husband and herself had not been very successful in collecting. They, therefore, preferred giving themselves. So saying, she counted out, from among a handful of silver and halfpence, ten sovereigns! The deeply-interesting scene of that day most strikingly reminded one of the people coming with their free-will offerings, in Moses' time, for the services of the tabernacle in the wilderness; and, in David's time, for the building of the temple at Jerusalem. One's heart on that most memorable day was filled to overflowing.

£250. A cheque from a baronet, the noble response to an appeal signed by nearly 3,000 parishioners.

£5 from a clergyman, the tenth of a legacy.

£100 anonymous. A letter was handed into the vestry just prior to the service on a Thursday evening. Upon opening it, it was found to contain ten £10 notes from an anonymous donor.

One penny sent by an aged widow in the neighbourhood of Salisbury, in proof of her love for the broadsheet, *Old Jonathan.*

£6 6s. The contents of boxes of a ladies' school, being the Monday-morning offerings of the pupils, who, in addition, were most persevering in their efforts with collecting-cards.

£20 from a friend, in acknowledgment of a successful enterprize.

£5 from an aged person. This gift was among his last acts.

£10 from an aged stranger, who sent a message to say, she would make it worth his while if the writer would go and see her. This kind friend is afflicted with blindness.

£5 from Manchester. The donor soon after passed into another world. In looking over the list, the writer cannot but be reminded of how many of the contributors are since dead.

£10 from Clifton. The donor responded to the appeal by return of post. In his note he expressed his hearty concurrence in the claims which it expressed. Though at the time in apparent health, in three or four days afterwards he was no more! Reader, "Whatsoever thy hand findeth to do, do it with thy might: for there is no work, nor device, nor knowledge, nor wisdom, in the grave whither thou goest" (Eccl. ix. 10).

3s. A poor farmer's wife.

£5. A thank-offering from a friend.

10s. The price of three doves.

£5 5s. from a dear brother-clergyman in Ireland.

£1 1s. from " A Fainting One," Navan post-mark.

£10 and £10 from an elderly gentleman, since deceased.

10s. 6d. A new year's gift from Rugby.

£10 and £10 and £10 from a lady, since dead. She was personally unknown to the writer.

Three of the congregation kindly collected, from most varied and distant channels, upon an average, £100 each; many others collected sundry smaller amounts.

10s. from a poor working man.

£17 10s., collected by the sickly wife of a toll-house keeper, a mile and a half from the church.

The writer has, in the preceding, cast his eye over the church-building list, and offered comments upon item after item as they have presented themselves, and so far as his memory would serve him. He will now proceed to take a similar passing glance at the various items contributed towards the erection of the schools. It has already been stated how the site was paid for, by the Churchwardens liberally contributing £125 each. The next sum standing upon the school-list is—

£50 contributed in the most cheerful manner by one unconnected with the Church of England, and who had also given two £10 to the church.

£20 from a relative of the above, of another persuasion, who had given £10 to the church, and who, in forwarding his donation, said, "I perfectly agree with the closing words of your Appeal, 'Freely ye have received, freely give.'"

Nine £10 contributed by the members of the Building Committee; one of these was the Churchwarden who had before given so handsomely.

£25 by one who had previously given £20 and £25 towards the church.

£4 7s. 4½d. The pence of pupils attending the ladies' school before referred to.

£1. Ps. xxxvii. 4, 5.

£2 3s. Sunday-school children's pence.

£3 presented to the writer in the street, by two ladies whose names are unknown.

£5 5s. The united gift of a few ladies of St. Matthew's congregation.

£10 from the gentleman referred to in a previous page, who "lets not his left hand know what his right hand does."

£10 from the late aged gentleman who gave two £10 towards the erection of the church, though residing some miles from the locality.

£20 from a merchant who had with the utmost readiness given a similar sum towards the church, though not residing in the parish.

£25 given voluntarily by merely an occasional hearer. [This lady, not having taken sittings, because very seldom resident in the neighbourhood, forwarded a £5 note to the writer, under the appellation of "conscience-money"—a very practical hint to those who occupy free sittings month after month, and year after year, when they have it in their power to pay.]

£10 and £5 from a resident in a distant parish, and who had contributed liberally to the building of the church.

£5 from a clergyman at Clevedon, who had also given to the church.

£5 from the elderly person in the North who had contributed £63 to the church building.

4s. 2½d. from a Bible class.

10s. from "A Little One, Manchester."

5s. from "A Servant, Islington."

£10 from the Mayor of Bristol.

£25 from a dear Christian friend in London, who had given three similar sums to the church.

£5 17s. collected by the wife of the toll-house collector before referred to.

£4 1s. 11d. Contents of a collecting-box.

1s. from a little boy.

£1 17s. from Cheltenham.

9s. 6d. Contents of another box.

10s. 5d. More Sunday-school pence.

15s. Sale of work by an invalid.

15s. 6d. The amount of a card taken by the above. She,

prior to her decease, took the liveliest interest in the parish, though a non-resident, and had never personally witnessed any of its operations.

£4 6s. 6d. collected by a sister of the above.

10s. from "A Friend to Schools."

£39 10s. collected by one of the friends who had previously collected £100 for the church.

£34 9s. collected by a second friend, who had likewise collected £100 for the church.

6d., 6d., 3d., and 1d., contributed by a poor woman from time to time after our Monday morning prayer meetings.

£1. Sale of work by an invalid lady who has been confined upwards of nine years to her bed, and who in various ways has contributed to the church and schools of this parish.

16s. 5d. Contents of the ladies' school-box again.

£1 from "Luther."

£1. "A New Year's Offering from M. T."

£2 from an ex-Mayor of Bristol. Given unsolicited.

£2 from a foreign Consul. Also unasked for.

1s. 6d. "A Friend in Sussex."

10s. 6d. from a working man.

£50 from an M.P.

£3. The Dean of Gloucester, with the expressed wish that he had it in his power to discharge the whole debt.

£10, £1 1s., £5, from a member of the congregation.

£15 8s. per *Gospel Magazine.*

£52 10s. each from two of the trustees, who had previously contributed £500 each to the church.

£10 from a gentleman who had contributed several times to the church building.

£5 from a distant clergyman.

1s. 6d. from Croydon.

£2 2s. 6d. Contents of another box.

£1 2s. 1d. Collected by a poor man.

£1 1s. from Freshwater.

10s. from a poor widow in Birmingham, left with ten children (eight wholly unprovided for), and who is resolved to devote a tenth of her income to the Lord. This was a part of £5 sent her by a relative from Australia.

£1 from a lady's companion in London who had again and again contributed to both church and schools.

£3. The produce of two washing machines.

3s. in farthings.

5s. "Sundry Servants in Ireland."

£5 from the Christian friend in London, who had previously contributed four £25 to the church and schools.

£57 10s. 2d. received in postage stamps.

£10 from a gentleman who had contributed £50 towards the church.

£2. Contents of a box.

7s. 3d. Children's pence.

£1 from a working man in London, who seeks to devote one-tenth of his earnings to the Lord.

10s. from a sailor's wife; a great invalid, suffering from heart-disease.

£10 from an elderly clergyman, who gave a similar sum to the church.

52 farthings, the year's savings of a little boy whose father died of consumption. His wish was to have presented these farthings to the Incumbent upon the day of the opening of the schools, but this the hand of death prevented. His last walk was to see the progress of the building. His widowed and exceedingly-delicate mother forwarded these farthings to the writer upon the day of the dear little boy's death. They were afterwards attached to perforated cards, with the fact just mentioned printed upon them, and were subsequently sold at a bazaar for 6d. each.

But it is time to close. The reader may naturally inquire, "What is the state of the case at present?" The answer is, that so extensive are the church and school buildings, that after an expenditure of upwards of £14,000—forwarded from all parts of the kingdom—a debt remains on the church of £700, nor is the tower yet completed. Nearly £300 likewise is required to meet the cost of the school buildings and fittings, considerable additions having been made to the original plans. Towards tl latter amount a gentleman who has already been a large cc tributor has voluntarily offered to contribute ten per cent., £30, provided the Incumbent can collect the other within s months from the 1st of October, 1863. Hence any who m feel they would like to contribute towards the work may n only have an opportunity of doing so, but will confer a lasti obligation upon the Incumbent of St. Luke's, Bedminst Somerset. The smallest contribution will be most gratefu received by him at his residence, Bedminster, or at the *C Press*, 117 to 119, Aldersgate Street, London.

[Since the foregoing was sent to the press, the writer h received intimation from two gentlemen altogether unconnect with the parish, and not belonging to the Church of Englan the one offering £20, and the other £10, upon condition that t sum above-named is collected within the time specified. The gentlemen had previously contributed £50 and £20 to the scho building fund, as well as £10 and £20 towards the erection the church.]

NOTE.

(EXTRACT FROM "MUSINGS," BY ALFRED.)

MY MOTHER'S PORTRAIT.

(See Frontispiece.)

I MUSE, dear mother, on thy sacred memory! Not many years ago, I lay, a helpless babe, beneath thy gentle care. Unconscious of each danger—scarce aware of oft-repeated wants, I reposed on thee—a poor dependant on thyself! 'Twas love—a mother's love—which prompted thee to watch thy infant; and, when that watching I contemplate, I cannot but admire His mercy who appointed *thee* my mother! But for His compassion—unmerited indeed—I might have been the offspring of a brute in human form, or subjected to thousand ills, from which poor, nature shrinks.

I muse with gratitude to Him, the Author of my being, whilst yet I trace thy gentle hand in leading me, a giddy child. I see thy watchful eye; I muse upon the deep solicitude which thou didst manifest on my behalf. Approaching boyhood—beginning now to show the seeds of disobedience—I see thee take my hand admonish, and again behold thee bow the knee, a suppliant for thy boy!

And now, a youth, I take my leave of home—the scene of early years. I stand and listen yet again to thy fond admonitions; yea, upon the eve of my departure, I hear thee say, as though it were but yesterday,—"*We are clear of your blood.*" And again I wave adieu as I see thee stand, with tearful eye, among the little group assembled on the shore whereon we parted.

Mother! thy prayers *were* heard! A gracious eye watched o'er me; and, though that parting scene was dark, and unnumbered evils seemed as though they would prevail, yet how wisely did our bounteous Benefactor order all! Forty years have rolled away since then, my mother, yet has mercy—boundless mercy—attended every step. Though vicissitude has marked my course, and trial and exercise have been my portion, yet compassions, infinite in number and degree, have ever been reserved for times of danger and necessity.

And now, my mother, I would turn to contemplate thyself! But a brief period, and thou wast here, a dweller in a house of clay! I see its outward form. This picture brings thee to my recollection. Each feature is thine own, my mother!—yes, it is thine own familiar face; it, too, bears marks of anxious "musings." But, my mother, all has ended well with thee. Thou didst dread "the cloud," I know. It approached with threatening. But see its issue. Did not Jehovah graciously fulfil His word, notwithstanding thy timidity? Who attended thee in early life? Who marked thy future course, and guided every step? Did not He, the Lord? And now arrived at hoary hairs—weak nature drooping—to whom canst thou be looking, but to Him? Cheer up, my mother—all is well. Jehovah will be faithful, though thou fearest. He'll crown thee yet with joy.

Ah! now the *mind* gives way. Intense solicitude through thy protracted pilgrimage, followed by that *quietude* which thou didst so often crave, brought a reaction that proved fatal to thy mental powers. Reason resigns her post; yet, 'tis well, my mother! Ah, my mother! mercy—rich mercy—mingles with the dispensation. It has brought us to resign thee at *His* bidding, who had need of thee. Thou wast *such a mother*—so tender, so solicitous—it was so true of thee, that

"E'en thy failings
Lean'd on virtue's side"

—that we know not what, but such a trial as that with which thou now art visited, could have made us willing to surrender thee. Instrumentally, it has made us willing that thou shouldst go to take possession of thy mansion in the skies. One interval of reason is all we crave. Yes, yes, He gives it, blessed be our God! Thine heart—thine eye—are manifestly upward; thanks to His name! We feared it not, yet 'tis pleasing in remembrance. Thy parting words—that outstretched hand—one long, yet brief adieu!—is grateful, and we part to meet again!

CPSIA information can be obtained
at www.ICGtesting.com
Printed in the USA
LVHW040024180422
716440LV00005B/454

9 783752 595468